A
MELANCHOLY
UNION

by

Monica Weber Babcock

Del Claire Press

ISBN: 978-0-578-33352-6

*Author's Note: I have italicized Irish words within the text. If unsure of the meanings, readers may consult the Glossary located at the back of the book -- wherein I have also included some of the more unusual expressions used throughout.

For my great-great-grandparents
Samuel and Julia.
Samuel, I hope you rest easy now that I have
told the story you have been nudging me to write
since I was ten.

Other books by Monica Weber Babcock:

Heartscape
Burden of Remembrance

PART ONE

1874

SAMUEL

Everywhere was blood.

Gushing and dripping from the riven bodies. Oozing from the tangled heaps of mangled legs and arms. Drip-drip-dripping into slippery crimson pools. Bespattering the grisly aprons of the surgeons. Clotting into purple gobbets upon their ghoulish tools of torture: probes and saws and tweezers and pliers.

Shutting my eyes to the dreadful scene I found 'twas all in vain. The gruesome sights would not be gone from my ravaged mind. And all the time my ears were after being rent by the din of artillery fire whizzing and booming not a mile yonder, and shaking the ground I sat upon as if 'twould tear the very world asunder.

Vying with that monstrous discord was the shrieking of anguished men. 'Twas like those hellfire tales the priests were always after sermonizing about. And it went on and on and on. Eternal damnation couldn't be any the worse.

Myself was after shaking like as if I was having the fits – my teeth a chattering and my chest a heaving. This only worsened the pain in my own left arm which was throbbing something fierce. Arrah, the red-hot pain seared the sinews down to my hand and up into my oxter.

Mercifully, after a time of exerting my utmost determination, I gathered my scattered wits back about me so as I could stop with the quaking. Mother of God, I was after being a sergeant! And so I compelled myself to present a brave picture to the suffering men lying all about me in that woeful barnyard.

You see, we injured ones had arrived there at the hospital barn during the previous evening, and by the aid of eerie lantern light we'd been promptly sorted. The ones bad off, but who could likely be saved with some well-applied stitches or the saw had been laid nearest the barn and tended to first. The poor souls who were past saving had been gently laid out beyond the barn and been provided with a semblance of comfort by the chaplain and a troop of caring ladies and lasses from the town.

The ambulating ones whose wounds could wait – myself was one of them – why we had settled ourselves wherever we could alongside the stone farmhouse and outbuildings.

Then just before dawn, the Rebel shelling started and continued all the livelong day. By one in the afternoon, the shells were falling so close that those of us who could walk were evacuated. We fled down a lane past a stone building that was serving as another hospital. 'Twas another scene of carnage, and those wounded there joined with us as we shambled on out of the worst of harm's way until we reached a bit of shade by a creek. We lay or milled about for hours until the shelling eased in late afternoon, when we returned to the big hospital barn.

All of this commotion only worsened our pitiful condition. My lungs which had been wrecked since early spring were burning something fierce what with the smoke and the haze of heat. Wheezing and coughing, I gratefully sat in a bit of shade alongside a stone outbuilding.

My arm was a-throbbing and I fearfully peered beneath the blood-caked strip of linen that'd been torn from my shirt to serve for a bandage. I cursed when I saw that the bleeding which had slowed to seepage had started flowing again. Though it pained me something fierce, I flexed it and to my relief found that I could still be after moving it to some little degree. The rebel ball had gone clean through my flesh and muscle just above the elbow, but thanks be to God, seemed to have missed the bone. I told myself that in truth, 'twas a trifling wound compared to the other poor fellas being tended to in the stone and timber barn serving for a hospital.

Well, as I said, I had slowly gathered my scattered wits about me and pulled myself into a semblance of my former self. By this time, 'twas late afternoon, and though I'd been suffering since I'd been shot the night before up on that damnable Cemetery Hill, some of these men had been suffering for nigh on two days. The fella sitting beside me had been fighting the Rebs over a wheat field all the afternoon before and he was sore distressed.

"Such a hot time of it we had," he told me, his eyes dazed. "No battle lines, just a tussle of men trying to kill one 'nother."

He was arm-shot too, but just above the wrist. I could see his swollen, bluish fingers poking out from the bloody bandage.

"There's pieces of bone sticking out," he told me, his bright blue eyes popping with fear. Then he noticed the stripes on my tattered coat, and commenced in an abashed tone. "I'm sorry Sergeant for I regret my faintness of heart. But I'm afeared to get called to that barn for they're surely going to lop off my hand."

His gaze traveled to the surgery tables that were all lined up at the front of the barn 'neath an overhanging eave where the surgeons had been working ceaselessly amputating countless arms and legs and feet and hands in a steady stream, throwing them onto ever growing piles of dead meat.

Though I shared his gloomy presagment as his hand looked to be perished already, I nevertheless tried to solace him.

"Arrah Bucko, aren't we all after feeling a bit faint of heart. But perhaps the surgeons can simply splint it, making it right as rain again."

"I'm afeared not, Sir" the fella said and shook his shaggy head. "You see, I can't move it neither, and the pain has turned to dead numbness." He touched it with his good hand and shuddered. "It don't feel a thing."

'Twas then, when he looked me straight in the eye, that I saw through the grime on his face that he was barely past boyhood and it aggrieved me, made me altogether sad.

"What's your name boyo?" I asked him, trying to take his mind from his suffering.

"Abner."

"Well Abner, I'm Samuel. And I too am leery of the patching up I'll receive in that barn yonder. But I'm also fondly pondering on my resulting respite from this damnable fighting."

"I 'spose that's the goodest way of looking at things." Abner said, then gave me the wary-eye.

"You sound like a Irisher to me, Sergeant Samuel."

"And so I am, God bless the mark. Originally from Antrim, but lately of Philadelphia."

"So, bein' as you're from Pennsylvania, your kinfolk must all be Unioners. What a blessing that must be to all be fighting under the same flag. Me, I'm from Kentucky and our folk are of two minds about this war. My kin is torn asunder just like the country itself." Abner's eyes took on a mournful look.

"You see Sergeant, I'm not just afeared for myself, but for my cousin Seth, too. His fate lies ever heavy on my mind. 'Specially after every battle. Him and me, well we was always close as two bugs in a rug. But we had diverse ideas about this here war and when Kentucky went for the Union, Seth went off to join the Rebs. For all I know he's the one coulda shot me." Abner's face was a picture of worry. "Or I coulda shot him -- kilt him even – in this battle or one of 'tothers I've been in."

"Sure and that's a tale of woe if I ever heard one," I replied.

Then we fell to silence. Spent, we sat on the hard ground, propped up against the outbuilding, beyond weary with the pain of body and mind. And all we could do was await our turn to be summoned to that barn of misery into which a steady stream of broken men were being hauled.

All the while, ambulances brought more loads of the newly wounded who were continually being brought in and sorted. The fierce battling was still going on, this being the third and final day of that most colossal engagement in that ill-fated town of Gettysburg.

As the hours wore on in that misery-laden barnyard, the reek of sweat and blood and vomitus and piss and shite all mingled into a revolting fug, rendering us barely able to breathe. All the while, the pitiless July sun scorched us raw. Our parched throats ached for water, though the buckets came round but rarely. Wretchedly we swatted at the merciless mosquitoes and the swarms of buzzing flies drawn to the filth, their tormenting an unendurable accompaniment to the abiding itch of the nits that perpetually resided in the hair on our noggins and inside our oxters and nether regions.

'Twasn't just Union soldiers being remedied at that barn either, plenty of secesh were brought there too. Anguished as we all were, we abided one another's company in peace, ignoring the bitter irony that we had inflicted this bodily harm upon one another.

And though one could say that the degree of my wound rendered me far better off than most of them who were destined for the surgeon's saw or the grave, I had another more grievous wound which was sorely raw and festering, one that couldn't be perceived even had I been sliced open by the most skillful surgeon. For 'twas way down deep inside my very soul where this vexatious, sorrowful grievance commenced to throb and seep its poison. I felt the venom fill my breast with a hot, fuming revulsion, and then it oozed up into my brain, rendering me stupefied, fuddled in the head, broken into bits.

And as I sat just yonder from that woeful barn, propped up against the stone summer kitchen awaiting my turn with the surgeon, I closed my eyes to shut out the revolting scene. Yet I couldn't silence the ghastly screams emanating from the barn or the discordant moans and cries of the soldiers waiting all around me. Nor could I ignore the whimpering of poor Abner by my side. Nor could I thwart the sickening stench that burned my nostrils and moiled my stomach. I felt hot tears coursing down my face, and though not a sob left my throat, the tears would not abate.

And 'twas then – in that bleakest moment of despair -- that I rose up out of myself, way up high into the air. Bird-like I wheeled to and fro, peering down on all that suffering torment with an astonished, queer sort of detachment. I glided for a good while as if on an abiding draft of air before I sank back down into my poor stinking body and was reacquainted to the horror of my dreadful state.

'Twas more than I could bear, and for the first time in my life, I willed myself to die, begged God to take me from this hellish earth. Prayed for my heart to stop beating, or the heat to stifle me to death, or the gangrene to set in and kill me. 'Twouldn't be the last time I would make such a plea for deliverance. For though 'tis been eleven years now since that woeful time at the hospital barn, I remain afflicted with this poisonous brokenness. Release through death has become nearly my daily supplication up to this very day.

In due course, Abner and myself were escorted to the barn amidst the shrieking and groaning of the men and the scraping of the saws. Poor Abner had the giving out under him of his legs and he pissed himself in his fright as he was led to one of the surgeons' tables under the barn eaves. I never knew what became of poor Abner, but I hope he survived, though I reckon he went through life one-handed.

By this time I was beyond the beyond, stunned as I was from the heat and the thirst, the pain and the sorrow and the despair. As I was directed to a corner of the barn by a window which let in the early evening light, I trod meekly as a lamb to slaughter, averting my eyes from the sufferers, shutting my ears to their unholy din. I was seated upon an upended crate beside a crude table fashioned from a large cupboard door balanced atop two barrels. Strewn upon this makeshift table were bottles and dressings and bowls and shears and pliers and probes and needles. Behind it sat a begrimed surgeon with bags the size of satchels 'neath his bloodshot eyes. Himself appeared as exhausted and disheartened as if he had borne the thick of battle.

Wearily, he motioned for me to place my injured arm upon the table, then he deftly cut away my bandage, exposing the gory mess. 'Twas as if myself was in a dream, for rather than being fearful, I was beguiled as I observed himself tending my own dear arm as if 'twas another man's entirely. The entry hole was a rather tidy little star of torn flesh, but when the surgeon lifted my arm to view the exit hole, I saw that it was all raggedy and gaping. Both holes had angry purply-red edges and were oozing clots of blood and pus.

"A bit of a mess in there," he said peering closely at the gaping end, "so I need to scour that debris out. But your bone is intact. As long as gangrene doesn't set in, looks like you'll be keeping your arm."

His assistant – a stout matron from the town -- offered me a measure of whiskey, apologizing in a soft, soothing voice, "I truly regret this is all I can offer you." Her soft gray eyes were full of motherly kindness. "But we are reserving the chloroform for the amputations and dire surgeries which have been utterly ceaseless."

"Yes Ma'am," was all I could muster in response as I was so far beyond myself in my dream-like befuddlement.

"Now hold still and bite down on this," the surgeon cautioned as he placed a wooden wedge in my mouth. "This is going to pain some, but only for a few minutes."

The kindly matron stood by my side, gripping my good hand with all of her considerable might whilst embracing me with her other arm, heedless of my filthy stench. Then the surgeon grasped my injured arm in a vise-like grip and, with a probe, plunged an iodine-soaked rag all the way through my wound, front to back.

Upon that first swipe, my brain fog lifted; I gasped and nearly vomited with the pain, and bit down so hard on that wooden wedge I thought I'd be after breaking all of my teeth. Yet I watched that surgeon work as he forced out bits of shirt linen and scraps of the blue wool of my uniform along with soot and pus and streams of fresh blood. All through my ordeal, that good woman held onto my hand for dear life whilst gently stroking my back, shushing and murmuring to me like I was her own suffering babe.

And though that beleaguered surgeon did a fine job of scouring my wound clean so that I never developed the dreaded sepsis or gangrene, and he displayed a solemn tenderness that I hadn't expected as he deftly stitched and dressed it, that good man could do nothing to draw out that poison that had begun to infest my splintered spirit.

As he finished his tending, I had a fit of wheezing and coughing that brought up a bloody dribble. As I struggled for breath, he handed me a bit of rag to whip my chin and peered at me and felt my forehead.

"How long have you had that cough?"

"Since February."

"And the fever?"

"'Tis been on and off."

"I don't like the sound of your lungs, nor the look of you. I'm keeping you here until the railroad is repaired and they can remove you to a hospital. You need further tending."

And though I should have been only delighted at the reprieve, I barely recollect leaving that place of anguish, my chest a-clattering and my arm a-throbbing like 'twas on fire.

I found myself being escorted around to the back of the hospital barn where I was led up the sloped ground to the upper floor that was already full of wounded men. I was directed to a far corner where I settled down and eventually drifted into a fitful slumber.

The next three days were a haze of pain and distress. All I can fully recollect is the incessant rain hitting the roof above me and thanking the good Lord I was inside, for many of the wounded were lying out in the rain and mud with naught a covering at all for the tents and supplies were bogged down on the roads clogged with retreating soldiers.

Finally, I was transported with other wounded to the train station where just five days previously I'd been facing the Rebel army. Arrah, but there was many a man missing an arm or a leg, a few missing an eye or half a jaw. Some were plainly at death's very door. And I knew I should be after thanking God for my good fortune. But not a bit of it. The state of me was that my wits were in smithereens, and I drifted as though I was a haunt with barely a care for the others.

That evening I rode that sorrowful freight train teeming with torn men, moaning in their misery. We lay upon beds of straw in packed freight cars and wended our way to Philadelphia – that city of plenteous hospitals. And though I'd called that city home for nigh on ten years, and my brother William lived there still, I felt no joy at the prospect of returning.

Presently, lulled by the rocking of the train, I lapsed into a fitful sleep. 'Twas then I dreamt about the finest of men, my comrade Ezra Cummings. The very man who had been beside me since before Second Bull Run was back with me again. His freckled face was sunburnt beneath his kepi which sat at its usual jaunty tilt atop his wild thatch of red hair. We two were back there again where we had been four days earlier, holding the high ground in the cemetery above that vexatious town of Gettysburg for the second day in a row.

And as Ezra and myself hunkered down amid the tombstones dodging rebel sniper fire, he persisted in being his steady, becalmed self. Yet, steady as he was, my man Ezra was always a one to laugh at a good joke. And so there he was chuckling and grinning at the antics of that *spalpeen* Ned McElwee who was peculiarly gifted with seeing the comical in every situation, no matter how dire. Being as we were positioned in a graveyard, Ned couldn't help but perceive the eerie irony of it and so he was after making jokes about how fitting 'twas to be battling in a graveyard because afterwards we wouldn't have to be after dragging the bodies anywhere, just dig holes right where they dropped and roll them in.

My man Ezra, why he was grinning and chuckling at Ned's jokes right up until a Minie ball burst his head wide open. Ezra's cheery face vanished in a spume of blood and brains, dousing me in its warm red splatter. Then poor Ezra's faceless body slumped to the ground, the gore of his head spurting blood, his freckled hands yet clutching his rifle.

I awoke howling and cowering on my bed of straw. All through the remainder of that hellacious train ride I commenced to relive Ezra's horrendous demise over and over again, as vivid as the first time: his grinning face bursting into fume; the salty, iron tang of Ezra's blood as it dripped all down my nose and passed through my very lips; his faceless body slumping to the ground.

These visions set my heart to shuddering and flip-flopping in my breast and myself to moaning and quivering like a crippled pup. I was drowning in a morbid sadness and an unabating terror that's been with me to this very day.

JULIA

Since the day I slipped from my Ma's worn-out womb, I've had myself a mighty portion of troubles. But the priests, them that knows all about God's mysterious ways, are always after telling us we shouldn't expect life to be nothing other than a woeful burden, for didn't the Blessed Virgin herself watch her own dear Son suffer and die upon the cross? So's all we can do is grit our teeth, put our heads down, and keep a going down that worrying road of troubles 'til God sees fit to take us to Himself.

Myself was the last of Ma's thirteen babies, so's I reckon it's no wonder I'm so fruitful myself, birthing nine of my own so far. 'Tho I solemnly pray that wee Maggie be my last. Most of Ma's babies wasn't long for this world. Born with the weight of the clay on them, they died near as soon as they came -- of fever or croup or belly flux, but mostly from want. We lived in a wee cottage in County Armagh, and though Pa spent his days scrabbling in the stingy ground, there wasn't never enough praties for our bellies nor turf for our fire.

Though wee and spindly, myself was ever after being a hale child. Ma was always naggling at me about my mulishness, but 'tis what's kept me a-going all these many years. I never give up to nothing or no one.

So's unlike all of Ma's feeble babies, I lasted, along with my darling brother Daniel. We two lasted even through the killing time of *An Gorta Mor*, back in the forties when all the praties rotted. Five long years we suffered from The Hunger, but I won't be after saying no more about that for 'tis a fog of pain and misery and nightmarish sights that I've heaved to the back of my mind and bolted fast behind a very stout door. 'Tis over and done with, and though I won't never forgive them fiendish *Sasanaigh* for trying to kill us Irish all off, I'll not let them memories slip out now except for to say that when *An Gorta Mor* was nearing its end myself and Daniel were the only ones left of our family, and we were but scarcely alive.

I'll not utter the cursed name of that devil of an Anglo landlord who caused this to be, bad *cess* to him. Arrah, doesn't myself know I must leave damnation to God, yet that *blaggard* surely deserves the eternal pangs of hell for murdering

Ma and Pa. For himself knew what he was about when he cast us out of our cottage, tumbling it over top of our scanty belongings and driving us out onto the road, making us to huddle in ditches like burrowing beasts. We couldn't even build our miserable selves a *scalp* in which to take a bit of shelter from the damp, for we had to keep a moving down the byways scavenging for nettles and the odd wild cabbage that wasn't froze out. The cold and the hunger and the misery carried Ma and Pa off in no time at all.

First 'twas Pa. We woke up one morning and he was stone cold and stiff, and we knew he was gone from this vale of woe. I'll never forget the face on him – all shriveled, his staring eyes sunk to the back of his head, his mouth gawping. Ma sobbed quietly as she gently set it all to rights.

We prayed a *An Gniomh Dolais*, a *Ar nAthair*, and a decade of *Se do bheatha a Mhuire*. Then Ma covered his poor worn-out face with a bit of linen she tore from her frock. We covered him up with whatever grass and dirt we could scrape together and left him there in the ditch wherein he died.

'Twas then Ma peered at me with them once lovely sea-green eyes of hers, now turned all dim and sunken in their sockets. She looked all the world like a ancient thing with her face all famished and skull-like.

She took my face in her boney hands and said to me, "Whatever happens *mavourneen*, don't youse and your brother never go to one of them workhouses. For they'll separate youse and set youse to breaking the rocks 'til youse fall into a heap. You'll not never be getting out alive. Them places are rank with the killing fever, the flux, and the typhus." And then she made me promise by God's holy name we wouldn't never go.

'Twasn't a fortnight later, Ma perished. Me and Daniel repeated our crude funeral for herself. At that time, myself was long about sixteen or so, and Daniel was maybe three years older. We didn't never know our ages for certain since not a one in my family could read nor write -- much to my lifelong shame, though 'tis neither here nor there in the final reckoning.

So when myself and Daniel found ourselves alone in the world, we steered our way clear of the scores of workhouses that was full up to the rafters with the suffering and the dying. Daniel had the notion to go east to Belfast in the feeble hope of finding employ in that great city with its shipyard and teeming docks and linen workshops.

"What are youse on about?" I scoffed. "They won't never hire us being Catholic."

"They won't be after knowing as we'll recite the *Ar nAthair* along with its Protestant ending just as good as any Anglo," he said with an Anglo turn of speech, for Daniel was always after being the grand mimic.

"But 'tis a mortal sin, Daniel! To deny the true faith and act the heretic will send us straight to hell!"

"God knows what 'tis that we truly believe and hold in our hearts, and He won't be after counting a bit of an act against us if it keeps us alive."

I was terribly afeared for our immortal souls, not sure at all if I could ever play at being the heretic, but I knew 'twas no good to argue with him once he'd made up his mind, for his noggin was after being as hard as my very own. 'Twas just his conscience 'twas more pliant than mine when it came to honoring the rules of our Holy Mother Church.

So, east we went, us two lost souls traipsing along in our foul, raggedy garments all crawling with the itchy nits. Ashamed I am to say it, but we was filthy as the day is long. Afore our cottage was tumbled, Ma was a great one for the cleanliness. Many there was who kept the pig or the cow in their cottage for to keep warm, but Ma wouldn't have a bit of it.

"Meagerness isn't no excuse for being dirty," she was always after saying. So there was always a bucket of fresh water by the door for to wash our faces and hands. Ma was forever checking our hair for the nits, running the comb through to be sure 'twasn't a stray one here or there. And on any fair, sunny day Ma put the bit of lye into the cauldron in the yard and boiled our clothes and blankets clean, then stretched them on the hedge to dry.

But arrah, with the tumbling of our cottage, those days of cleanliness were long gone. So here we was, myself and my brother, filthy as pigs, traipsing down the byways, grubbing for the bit of food and any form of crude shelter along the way. The tinkers of times afore The Hunger would've looked to be very lords and ladies by compare. And 'twas only through a strange and fearful occurrence that myself and my brother survived.

We was hobbling down the road in a muddled state, so worn down with the hunger and the damp and the grief when of a sudden there appeared a newly reaped field. 'Twas mostly just the moiled-up soil, but here and there just setting in that field like precious jewels was the odd plump turnip that'd been overlooked, just waiting to be eaten.

Astonied, we stared at one another for we couldn't be after believing there was hearty food so easy for the taking. And though we were on our last legs, we fairly scampered into that field and fell upon them turnips, shoving them into our gobs like as if they was Moses's saving manna which in truth they was, gnawing away not minding the mud that we swallowed right along with them lovely things.

I tried to bide my time and chew it up good so's I wouldn't be after getting the stomach grip or the belly flux, for many's the time I'd seen a famished one no sooner bolt a bit of food down than his sore belly made him to vomit it back out. But 'twas hard to go slow when my stomach was crying out for to be filled. Those muddy turnips tasted lovely beyond the beyond after so long a time of famine, and though I chewed them up right good I made short shrift of them.

Once our bellies was full up -- which didn't take but two turnips apiece since our innards was so shrunk from the hunger -- we stumbled through the length of that field, picking up them few darling abandoned turnips. We stowed them into the sack Daniel was after toting for to give us the bit of cover at night.

We was just after heading back to the road with our sack justly full when we heard a angry shout from behind. We turned to see a man astride a horse, galloping right toward us as if his very life was at stake. When he reached us, he bellowed in his drunken Anglo tongue, "You damn vermin, I saw what you did! Drop that sack and get off my land before I whip the two of you and haul you off to the magistrate!"

He held his horsewhip aloft as if to strike us. His stout face under his shiny top hat was as red as his rich velvet coat, and his eyes was popping out his head like as if he had the apoplexy. I couldn't think how the loss of a pittance of turnip leavings could make a one like himself so angry - - a one so vastly plump with means to dress as finely as himself was -- unless he be drunk as a lord, which himself was clearly after being.

Daniel, always a one who could charm the devil himself what with his flaxen curls and Ma's lovely sea-green eyes, smiled sweetly at the *blaggard* and apologized mightily. Then he dutifully asked, "Sir, could we be after keeping just a meager portion of what we've gathered seeing as how dear they are to us who are suffering so from the hunger?"

But that black-hearted scoundrel just sneered at us and let loose a string of cursing I'll not repeat but 'twas fit to shame the vilest sailor. Then that brute leaned down from his saddle and commenced to savagely lash at my brother with his horsewhip.

Daniel darted 'neath the horse's head to dodge the lash, and all this uproar startled the jittery beast who reared up, flinging his rider to and fro like as if he was no more than a overstuffed ragdoll.

The *louser* snatched at the horse's mane to steady himself, but being so far gone in his cups he only flailed and wobbled about which startled the beast all the more and made him to rear again. This time the more wildly.

The scoundrel squawked as he lost his grip and flew high into the air. Then didn't he flop head first to the ground and lie there all in a crumple. Himself wasn't after moving at all, so Daniel and myself drew up close. 'Twas then we saw his eyes popped and staring out a noggin so awry it lay sidewise his crookedy broken neck. Stone dead was he. That begrudger wouldn't no longer be after caring about us snatching his odd turnips that set like a lord's feast in our sack.

I couldn't help but wonder was it God's very hand that toppled that greedy *louser* off his steed to dish out his just desserts and keep ourselves fed for the nonce. But I joined Daniel in crossing ourselves and reciting a *An Gniomh Dolais* as was our Catholic duty, even upon the death of a heretical Anglo.

Then Daniel grabbed the horse's reins and turned the creature back the way it had come, giving its haunch a mighty slap. Away it ran to home. My brother said that a one would surely be along directly searching after the dead Anglo, so we must be off and on our way. He picked up the sack of lovely turnips and off we traipsed toward the road.

Then Daniel stopped. "Bide here," said he, and trudged back to the body. He knelt down and fumbled with the dead man's clothing.

Troubled, I tramped after him and saw that he was digging through the scoundrel's pockets. He pulled out his hand and there lay a heavy gold watch worth a king's ransom.

"Arrah, Daniel!" I cried, seeing what he was about. "Surely youse can't be after stealing from a dead man?"

Thrusting the treasure back inside the dead man's pocket and without looking up he said, "I'll not be a common bandit and strip him of his trinkets. I'm only after taking his money for to buy us food. He don't need it no more."

"But that's thievery!" I cried.

Daniel stood up, thrusting the notes and coins into his pockets. "God and the Holy Church won't be after holding it a sin when 'tis the only thing keeping us from the grave."

And as I saw the truth in his words, I said no more; yet in the quiet of my soul I asked God's forgiveness once again and recited a *An Gniomh Dolais* for to cover the both of us.

On we trod toward Belfast, Daniel clutching our meager sack of turnips as if it held a lord's feast, which indeed it did. Stopping every mile or so along the way to rest, we'd gnaw one more turnip to brace ourselves. Once, Daniel emptied his pockets and counted all the money. I kept still as I could see he was deep in rumination.

As we neared the city, Daniel turned to me and said, "Sure, once we're in Belfast we'll find the modest lodging and buy the milk and the bacon and the loaf of good bread."

My mouth watered at that. Daniel's sea-green eyes shined with a light I hadn't seen in many a month. I thought 'twas the promise of shelter and food, but I soon learnt he was after thinking on a far grander plan than soothing our bellies for a time whilst we searched for employ.

"And after we've had the bit of rest and our bellies are good and stuffed," said he a-grinning away, "we'll buy our passage for America."

SAMUEL

Myself was in such a sorry state when our train full of the battle-maimed arrived in Philadelphia that I scarcely recollect it. Nor can I recall the particulars of my ensuing conveyance to the foremost soldier's hospital, Cuyler in Germantown. 'Twas in that vast place of suffering where my wounded arm was tended to along with my hacking, wheezy lungs.

What I do recollect is that I no sooner got through the door of that woeful place when I endured an inept scrutiny by a rheumy-eyed surgeon. Three sheets to the wind was he, with the reek of whiskey coming off him, fresh over stale. Himself was nearly reeling, so much in his cups was he. With his bleary, bloodshot eyes, he peered at my bandaged arm, squinted into my eyes, had a peek down my gullet, and thumped my chest. He then mumbled an order to the attendant who led me to a ward full of my fellow soldiers suffering varying gradations of ailment, mutilation, and dismemberment.

At the sight of all of that misery, my heart commenced to galumphing and my chest to heaving. So severely was my heart racketing away in my chest, that my ribs seized up and I couldn't catch my wind. A terrible buzzing took hold of my head like as if 'twere a hive of bees, and myself was rendered so feeble that I was nearly falling down what with the blackness dropping down over me and the giving under me of the legs as I tottered after the orderly to my assigned cot.

I slumped down upon it in relief, closed my eyes, but no sooner caught my breath than I commenced to coughing and gagging. I grabbed my handkerchief out my pocket and spit up a big gout of bloody rheum. Once my coughing spell subsided, I concerted all of my faculties on slow, easy intakes of breath to slacken my flip-flopping heart and quiet my head which was still a-buzzing. After a time, the buzzing ceased and my heart slowed down to a more natural rhythm. I opened my eyes, whereupon I found myself facing the blind side of a one-eyed young lad.

He was sitting there in the cot beside mine with the top right side of his head all stoved in and there was a gaping hole where his ear had once been. 'Twas dreadful to behold his mutilated head, yet it prompted a morbid fascination in me and I gawked at it utterly amazed that a fella could survive like that with only half a noggin. He must have felt my unsolicited attention; forthwith he turned his half-head toward me.

Jolted was I by the loveliness of what remained of that boy's face which only rendered the missing portion all the more gruesome and his plight altogether more tragic. His enduring half a face was framed with red-gold curls, his one remaining eye was large and the vividest of blues. His nose, partially gone, still bore the remnant of one chiseled nostril whilst his unspoiled mouth was almost girl-like in the curve and fullness of the pink lips. Still bearing the stamp of childhood, the lad couldn't have been more than seventeen, and I mourned for his mother's sure sorrow at her lovely son's horrific maiming.

Forthwith he responded to my impudent gawking by fixating his remaining eye on me; it gleamed with madness. Chastened, I looked away, but not soon enough. Himself commenced to bellow at me in a Dutchy tongue similar to what I'd heard so often in the Eleventh Corps which was rife with immigrants from Prussia and the like.

For a time I ruefully gazed down into my lap since I justly deserved the reprimand. But growing ever more embarrassed at his scolding, I looked up and away down the length of the room, planning my escape.

That's when I noticed a few cots down was a nurse who was dressing a wound. She turned to look our way, and as the enraged half-headed boy's rebuking me became loud enough to raise a graveyard's tenants, she left off her wound-dressing and came over to becalm him.

Arrah, she was a pretty young thing with lively dark eyes, ivory skin and rich auburn hair pulled up under her crisp linen cap. She gently took Half-Head by the hand, tenderly turned his ruined face toward her own lovely one and said in a soothing voice, "There's nothing to fear, Hans. You've got a new neighbor and he is a fine upstanding Union soldier like yourself. So all is well. All is well."

Herself gently brushed the curly golden locks out of his solitary eye and peered into his tragic half a face with the smile of an angel which brought about the desired calming effect. I don't know that Hans understood her words, but he clearly understood their intent. He presently quieted down to a soft muttering, and the lovely nurse nodded and smiled at me then returned to her station attending the wounded. My eyes followed her pretty self the entire way for she was a heavenly sight amidst all the ugly misery of that cursed place.

As Hans Half-Head softly nattered away in his native Dutchy, I removed my brogans and situated myself upon my cot. Then I turned to view the cot on my other side, resolute to demonstrate the utmost courtesy to whomever unfortunate I found residing there. On that cot lay the top half of a fella. The poor devil was missing both of his legs entirely so not even a remnant of a stump remained. I was after gawking again, wondering if that fella could even relieve himself what with so much of him missing. But this time my discourtesy mattered not a jot, because what was left of himself lay with his eyes closed. He was still as death.

"Arrah," I said to myself, "I've been set down amidst the halves!" 'Twas then I reckoned I misjudged the sot of a surgeon who surveyed me upon my arrival. Though himself was after being drunk as a lord, he yet detected what was at the core of my wounding -- that I was riven, albeit on the inside, half my wits gone astray surely as any common half-wit.

I turned from pitiful Half-Man and peered across the way at the cots on the other side, but couldn't gather much about the inhabitants, other than most appeared to be missing sundry parts.

These mutilated bodies harkened me to ponder on gruesome battlefields, to the countless maimed and dead I'd seen throughout the last two years. And though I tried to waylay his face from appearing, I could not keep Ezra away. I relived his awful demise for the umpteenth time, and my heart set to pounding and my chest to heaving and myself to sobbing. I knew 'twas unmanly, but I couldn't catch ahold of my wits enough to cease. The blackness enfolded me, and 'twas fortunate I was in my cot for I'd have surely fallen down.

Woeful beyond measure, I closed my eyes to be shut of it whereupon I fell into a slumber. I know not how long I slept, but I awoke to a most distressing intrusion -- the whiff of ghastly putrefaction. Startled, I believed myself to be back on the battlefield. I turned my head to and fro, took in my surroundings, and felt a small measure of security. Then with my snout in the air, I swiftly determined that the miasma was wafting from the right, from Half-Man himself who was rotting away.

His lifeless trunk seemed to have sunken deeper into the cot, and his face, which had turned as yellow as a buttercup, glistened with oily sweat. I knew that stink – 'twas the commencement of the death stench of gangrene, soon to become overpoweringly noxious. Once experienced it can never be forgotten as the reek is indescribably putrid, mingling the worst of all imaginable odors: rotten meat, shite, old blood, and pus all stirred together and steamed into the vilest fug. The poor rotting fella was at death's very door, but as he was clearly past caring I could only be after feeling sorry for myself having to put up with his intolerable stink.

Fortuitously, the surgeon was heading my way. And beside him walked the charming young nurse who had becalmed poor Hans Half-Head. They stopped aside my cot and the surgeon smiled at me, seemingly oblivious to my neighbor's stench.

"I'm Doctor Clark and this is Nurse Fields," he shook my hand in greeting. "I hope you are settling in nicely, Sergeant."

"Perhaps I could be doing just that if 'tweren't for this poor fella here," I nodded toward Half-Man. "Can you be after seeing to him? The death stench of gangrene is coming off him something terrible."

"He's past saving," sighed Doctor Clark who was unperturbed by the foul fug that had myself near to retching. "So I'll see to you first."

He smiled at me most woefully and commenced his inspection. He unbandaged my arm and peered at my wound, gently felt around the edges and told me it was showing no sign of putrefaction. He then ordered Nurse Fields to bathe it with iodine and apply a fresh dressing. Meantime, he bared my breast and brought forth from his prodigious satchel a long wooden listening device, placing the flat end upon my chest and inserting his right ear into the cupped end.

Whilst he was duly absorbed in listening to my rales and thumping my chest, I furtively watched the lovely doe-eyed Nurse Fields. She couldn't have been more than twenty years of age. As I watched her tend my arm and felt her gentle ministrations, an unbidden stirring filled my loins and I hastily pulled the sheet up to hide my rising mortification.

"Now cough," ordered Doc Clark.

I obliged, hoping 'twouldn't set off a spate. It did, but leastways 'twas a short one.

Putting his listening device aside he inquired, "How long have you had the coughing and wheezing?"

I told him since February, commencing directly after the dreadful Mud March in late January when we slogged through icy rain for five frigid days and nights. At that, his mild face took on a black look and he mumbled something to the tune of, "Idiotic generals, damn fools killing our own hale boys."

Then he instructed Nurse Fields to make certain I was provided with additional victuals of warm broth three times a day, bread with an extra slathering of butter, two eggs a day, and a dose of opium each morning and night until the coughing subsided, to which she answered, "Yes, Doctor" in her lilting way.

As she finished tending my arm, Doc Clark bid me well, shook my hand once again, and turned his attention to Half-Man. After feeling for the fella's pulse and applying the wooden hearing device to the slackened chest, he sighed and pulled the sheet over the dead yellow face. With a catch in his voice, he instructed Nurse Fields to see to the soldier's removal as soon as possible. She nodded, finished dressing my arm, and hurried off.

In short order, two darkies from the death patrol came to fetch Half-Man. They had covered their noses and mouths with neckerchiefs in a feeble attempt to ward off his stench. They swathed his reeking half-corpse up tightly within his fouled bed linens. But when they lifted the bundled cadaver from the cot, they disturbed the gaseous pockets which had collected under the bloated, blackened skin at his loins, releasing the worst of the revolting fug. The noxious wave assaulted me and caught in my throat, making me to retch. Themselves handling the body must have had a sore time keeping from heaving whilst they hauled Half-Man away. That fug of deathly rot hung in the air for hours afterward, lingered in my snout for days, making my appetite to suffer a downturn.

That evening, I taxed myself to put aside my morbid thoughts and write my brother a letter. I feared he'd seen my name in the list of casualties at Gettysburg, and I wanted to ease any worry he might be harboring on my account. I informed him that I'd survived, was on the mend, and was indeed in hospital in Germantown Philadelphia as the postmark disclosed. But I requested he not visit me just yet. I made the excuse that I needed sustained rest so my arm and lungs could mend properly, but in truth 'twas because I wasn't in my own mind and didn't want himself to see me so distempered. I told him I'd let him know when I was hale enough for visitors.

My familial duty fulfilled, I settled in and set my sights on recovery. As the weeks wore on in that place of misery, my arm slowly mended and my coughing diminished, but my melancholy and apprehension worsened, making me to grow more fuddled, enfeebled, and agitated. Days, I listlessly shambled through the hospital wards only to witness multitudes of once-hale men decay away. Their shrieks, more piercing than any *banshee*'s, battered my ears; their outpourings of piss and shite and vomitus and rot poisoned the air, stinging my nose and gullet.

Nights, I dreamt of Ezra – his freckled, grinning face bursting into bloody spume, his body slumping to the ground. 'Twasn't long before I was after having spells of overwhelming agitation that commenced my heart to battering so powerfully that I'd be swooning, and then a kind of blindness and deafness would sweep over me when all went black and silent, like as if a smothering shroud swathed my head. In my panic, I'd take to gulping great gasps of air which would lead to painful coughing fits.

'Twouldn't be long before an attendant would find me where I lay crumpled on the floor and, seeing the state of me, lead me like as if I was blind man back to the safety of my cot. Subsequently, the coughing would abate and the black silence finally lift, yet I'd be all atremble with terror and begging God and all the saints to save me from it happening again.

Though Dr. Clark took note of my declining state of mind and tried his best to tend to my panicky bouts, ordering cool compresses and bedrest, these ministrations were ineffectual. He informed the surgeons in charge that, while my wounded arm was nearly mended and my chest had shown improvement, I was sorely impaired by my lingering fits of heart thrashings and my petrifying occurrences of blindness and deafness. But the surgeons in charge would have none of it. They chose to put it all down to my lack of fortitude as my mind sickness was beyond their ken to fathom or remedy.

Yet even those *amadans* had to admit what was as plain as horseflies on shite -- that they couldn't return me to my regiment as enervated and unserviceable as I was. So, they put their *eejit* noggins together and pronounced that all I needed was a wee bit more bedrest and warm broth to make me altogether right as rain again.

They kept me there at Cuyler for nigh on three months, but I got no better. In desperation, those charlatans decided a three-week furlough might be just the thing to bring me back to myself.

So it came about that at the end of September of '63, my brother William arrived at Cuyler in his buckboard. He hadn't seen my homely self in two years and upon beholding me, he looked sorely taken aback.

Quickly recovering himself he said, "You're after looking a bit weary there Bucko, but we'll soon have you dancing to the reels again."

Even so, his voice was quaky and telltale tears shimmered in his eyes, and I pondered on what a frightful sight I must have made.

He embraced me warmly, picked up my haversack, and loaded it and myself into the buckboard. As we rode along, William tried his utmost to converse with me, catching me up on family tidings and such. But my benumbed mind couldn't take it in, his voice was just a nattering to me, so I couldn't respond in any meaningful way.

After a bit he said, "Arrah Samuel, I'm like to be gabbing your ear off when, weary as you are, all you want is some peace. I'll leave off my blathering now."

I tried to smile at him, and we travelled the rest of the way in unnatural silence. My mind was discomposed, wandering hither, thither, and yon, unable to settle on my change in circumstance. I was powerless to connect with my own dear brother who had accomplished a great deal in his adopted country while I had only failed.

He'd always been a bright, solid lad, with an aptitude for mechanical things and our Daddy's cheery disposition. When he first came to Philadelphia, he'd been a common laborer laying train tracks. But through his sharp wits, he worked his way up until in due course, he got himself the grand job of train engineer. This job not only paid a pretty penny, but when the war came, it exempted William from the draft which was a blessing as he had the wife Lydia and four small children in his keeping.

By autumn of '63 when he came to fetch me from Cuyler, himself was earning sufficiently to provide a cozy dwelling for his brood in Manayunk, a district of hardworking folks who lived in modest comfort. And when we arrived at his doorstep on Cotton Street, I perceived that his dwelling was one in a row of tidy houses leading down toward the riverfront.

As soon as we entered the door, Lydia came running to greet me with a truly heartfelt smile lighting up her lovely face. "Why Samuel, I've been so looking forward to seeing you again!" she exclaimed, embracing me warmly.

I'd always been fond of Lydia. Thoroughly American she was as she'd been born and reared in Philadelphia. Her mammy's people had come from Tipperary, whilst her Daddy's folks were after being from Holland a way back in the seventeen-hundreds. I didn't hold that against her as she was sweet as they come.

The four wee ones -- stepping stones from age seven on down to a mere tottering babe – gathered around their mammy and peered at me in an enquiring way, the smallest one warily hiding behind her mammy's skirt.

"Terrence, Abigail, you remember your Uncle Samuel," Lydia chirped to the two eldest.

Terrence gave me a little nod while Abigail stared at me wide-eyed.

"And these two," Lydia informed me, "are Patrick -- who was just a babe last time you saw him-- and our little Sheila."

"What a fine brood you've got yourselves," I said, trying my best to smile at the little ones so as not to scare the bejabbers out of them.

Lydia, always a sensitive soul, directly perceived my fatigued discomfort and said, "Oh but Samuel, you must be exhausted and famished! And here I am chattering away when you'll have plenty of time to get acquainted with the children later." Then she turned to William. "Dearest, please show your brother to his room so he can rest before dinner."

I was beyond grateful to Lydia for affording me the chance to have a few moments to myself, for I was having quite the time trying to keep the wits about me, what with my new surroundings after so many months in that wretched hospital. William led me to the cozy back room, where he deposited my haversack aside the washstand.

"There's fresh water here in the pitcher and bowl," he said, "and a razor and soap for you to be using whenever you see fit. I'll let you rest a wee bit then fetch you when dinner's ready. 'Tis anything else you're after needing?" He peered at me with sad, pitying eyes that nearly tore the heart right out my chest.

"Arrah no," I told him. "Everything is grand. Sure 'tis I'm right fatigued, but a wee sleep will do me wonders."

William smiled and left me to myself, and all I can recall is sitting upon the bed, utterly befuddled, trying to gather my bestrewn wits about me.

Now my brother and myself have always been as close as two peas in a pod, but all I can recollect of that three-week sojourn in his home is that I couldn't settle down at all. I could barely eat even though Lydia, God bless that lovely woman, went to great pains to cook roasts and biscuits and buttered praties and pies. And the din caused by the children agitated me something fierce.

I do recall a sorrowful looking William bidding me converse with him on several occasions, but I can't recollect a thing he said, only that I wanted no part of it. His voice was a clattering I couldn't comprehend nor abide. It was like as if I was locked away inside a glass box and no one could get through to me, but they expected me to converse in a normal way which I could not do. So restive was I and so mired in deepest melancholy that I wished only to run far away from everyone and burrow into a deep, dark hole and not ever come out, just sleep and forget like some hibernating creature but for all of eternity.

I loved William more than anyone -- we were blood – so this peculiar estrangement from him troubled me something terrible. His palpable distress at my drawing away beset me with the guilts, and knowing what a loathsome burden I had become to himself and his family, I heartily yearned for the peace of the grave. 'Twould do us all a kindness if I was gone.

So, many was the time in those three weeks that I took up that razor lying aside the washbowl and deliberated about slicing my throat. (I'd once seen a deranged rebel whom we were after capturing pull out his bowie knife and dispatch himself in this way. Though terribly bloody, 'twas quick and efficient.) Knowing that my poor bloodied remains wouldn't be a proper sight for William nor his brood to find, I decided that when 'twas time, I'd go on out the road down the riverfront and do the deed where a stranger would be after finding me.

It came to be that one day when I was beset with the blackest of melancholia and unease that I went on down the riverbank intent on my purpose. As I stood there pondering on the proper place, didn't a wee lad run up to me inquiring if I'd seen his little brother about. Sorely distressed was he as he divulged how he'd lost track of him while they'd been fishing. Before I could answer, didn't the little lost fella come running up laughing, and the look of relief on the older brother's face was beyond joyful. The lads scampered off, the older one scolding the younger for worrying him to bits, but the incident left me with the sure knowledge that my doing myself to death would cause my older brother untold pain. I pocketed the razor and trudged back to William's house.

Arrah, what had driven me to this deepest despair was that I couldn't grasp why my own brother's company was not after helping me, why I was still so broken even while in his tender care. William had always looked after me. We had shared a lifetime of gladness and sorrow going back to our boyhood in County Antrim.

Ours had been a loving family. 'Twas just the two of us lads, William being the older by two years. I took after our mammy who was tall and spare with piercing blue eyes and honey-blond hair. Even though she took sick and died of the galloping consumption when I was but eight years old, I vividly recall her lilting laugh and quick mind. Tenderly would she sing to William and myself, clasping us close, merrily calling us "my darling boyos, my *acushlas*." And even when we were up to making the mischief, she would laugh and tell Daddy, "Arrah Thomas, but aren't these two *spalpeens* of ours after giving their mammy grief again! Whatever shall we do?"

And Daddy would be after playing along, laughing and jesting, "I think I'll just take the two of them out the road and down the river and leave them for the faeries who like nothing better than to charm the handsome, wayward children away to take for their own."

"Now that's after being a grand idea!" Mammy would say. "These troublesome boyos of ours will take right to the faeries' tricky ways."

And we'd all be laughing. For though many of the country folk still harbored a credence in the magic of faeries and the portentous power of banshees, Daddy and Mammy had taught us that those creatures did not in truth exist, but were just so much superstition.

Alas, there were also troubling times when Mammy suffered spells of dark melancholy; she would go silent and her gaze would mist over and she would drift away off somewhere sad and mournful for a time where we couldn't reach her. These times frightened William and myself, for we were after fearing there would come a time when she wouldn't return to being her own dear self.

But Daddy would assure us that 'twas only because Mammy needed the odd time to mourn their first babe, a wee lass named Mary Rose who died scarce two months on this earth. She'd gotten the fever and belly flux and died in Mammy's arms. Daddy said when they buried Mary Rose, they buried a piece of Mammy's heart along with her.

Those times of Mammy's melancholy were hard, but the very worst time was when Mammy caught the consumption. It took hold of her and carried her off swiftly. The fever spots appeared on her cheeks, she was wracked with the coughing, and soon she grew thin as a rail. Within three months she was spitting up gouts of blood and was so weak she had to take to her bed where she died within a fortnight. Her demise was a terrible blow from which we never recovered. Our Daddy neither.

He was a kind, gentle man with soft brown eyes and an easy laugh. Born to the life of a tenant farmer, his soul was that of a poet and a *seanchaidhe* who loved to be after telling a good tale. In happier days, he regaled us with many a one. And Daddy was always one to love the music; he sang with a lilting tenor voice while thumping away on his *bodhran*.

And though a country lad, he was educated thanks to his Uncle Emmett a Jesuit priest who taught him to read and write whilst he was a mere boyo. This uncle had been after owning several books, a true rarity, and when he died, he left them to Daddy: a copy of Donne's poetry and Meditations (heretic though Donne was, Uncle Emmett claimed that Donne's writings were Godly); two volumes of Shakespeare -- one of his comedies, the other of his tragedies; and a history of Irish myth. Daddy revered these books and read them often, and he employed them in teaching William and myself how to read and write. And so we were after learning the loftiest of language.

Though my brother and myself were thick as thieves, we'd always been different creatures in disposition. William was ever after being the cheerful, practical one, loved anything of a mechanical or mathematical nature, and kept his mind resolutely focused on his doings. Arrah, I was ever after being dreamy, ever after woolgathering when I should have been paying attention to the goings-on around me. Daddy would be explaining to William and myself something of import, then look at me with an expectant look. I'd suddenly come to my senses having no idea what he'd said.

"For the love of God, Samuel," Daddy would say, "sure you were off and aways somewhere in that dreamy noggin of yours again. Always behind like the tail of the cow!" And then he'd grin and tousle my hair, so I knew he wasn't cross, whilst William just harrumphed and rolled his eyes.

Accordingly, William paid solemn attention during our Daddy's reading and writing instructions as he considered these skills to be necessary tools, whilst I positively lived for the book reading as it took me away to faraway places and set my restless mind to all manner of imaginings. Every moment spent with my snout in those books was a delight! I would gobble up the words like they were vital sustenance. Words! Are there any such lovelier things? To be strung together into such pleasing resonances and rhymes! Language is surely like celestial music. Many's the time when the cadence of a charmingly arranged verse has sent a delightful shiver down my spine. In that way, my soul was akin to my Daddy's, always stirred by the poetry, so I read and reread his books until I knew many a line by rote.

Well, the three of us, though missing Mammy something fierce, nonetheless shared some glad times until my tenth year when the agonizing blow of *An Gorta Mor* assailed us along with all of our countrymen. For ages, we Irish had lasted quite fitly on our nourishing fare of praties augmented with buttermilk, cabbages, and the odd piece of bacon. But in 1845, a massive potato blight the likes of which we'd never before suffered descended on us of a sudden. One day we had lovely firm, white praties, and the next day they'd all turned to oozing tar, their rotting stink hanging heavy over everything like a death shroud. Which was precisely what 'twas.

For the next five years, the blight plagued our pratie crops so severely that we suffered the agony of perpetual hunger. Black '47 was the worst when we had not a single pratie, just the few turnips and cabbages we could scavenge along with the nettles. Daddy had to sell our cow and two pigs to pay the rent on our meager plot, so there was no more buttermilk to be had, let alone the odd piece of bacon. 'Twas only the Anglo landlords who were after keeping livestock for to breed and sell to the English for a pretty penny. And they set guards around their lands to watch against thievery by the hungering multitude.

In truth, our fertile soil and soft rains provided plentiful food in addition to the praties. There was the wheat and the barley and the oats and the corn; the lush grass that fattened the cattle and the sheep. But ever since the *Sasanaigh* stole our land, our bounty was never ours to enjoy. Even during *An Gorta Mor*, all that abundance that could have soothed many a starving Irish belly and saved countless lives was still being loaded onto the ships headed for

England same as usual to feed their overstuffed lords, bad *cess* to them.

An Gorta Mor slew a million of my countryfolk outright. And of the other million compelled to flee to America and Canada in the teeming, typhus-ridden coffin ships, thousands more died and were buried at sea. This death or exile of two million Irish souls was *Sasanaigh* barbarity at its worst, unforgiveable as well as piteous since the famine could have been so easily remedied by keeping Irish bounty in Ireland. But English greed prevailed.

'Twas how it has always been since the time of the fiendish Tudors, most especially that vile Bloody Bess who seized our fruitful land in her grasping claws. Coldblooded she-devil that she was, she not only stole the bounty of our soil, she stole the land itself – taking Irish domains away from their rightful owners and bestowing them as tokens on her cunning flatterers. And 'tis the descendants of those Anglo landowners who have kept the Irish as downtrodden as any darkie slave. For three-hundred years now, those lousers have left us only praties whilst scanting us of all of the other plentiful crops our bountiful land provides.

Yet even *An Gorta Mor* wasn't enough to soften the black heart in the *Sasanaigh*'s breast. All through The Hunger, those *blaggards* couldn't be stirred by common charity to let us keep even the meagerest portion. They were not about to let the native folks' suffering and dying for lack of food cut into their profits.

Now that other devil's handmaid who has held the cursed English throne far too long whilst spawning a whole litter of whelps to continue in her wicked footsteps – the Famine Queen Victoria – was not about to step in. Ignoble as her ancestors with ice water running through her veins, she has always treated the Irish as rebellious savages rather than acknowledge our bravery in fighting to reclaim a nation that is rightfully ours.

That loathsome she-beast was in truth overjoyed at the prospect of whittling down our bothersome population. She and her man Trevelyan responded to our mass starvation by sending us tons of gravelly Indian corn, so coarse the pigs would've turned up their snouts at it. It hurt the teeth and produced belly pains worse than the hunger it was meant to gratify. We suffered the agonies of the damned as it raked through our poor tender bowels until we shite it out in bloody, undigested gobs.

By the time Black '47 came around, that bastard Lord Russell had taken over where Trevelyan had left off. Even more begrudging, he stood aloof as my countrymen perished by the thousands along the roads and in the fever-ridden workhouses. Folks were so gaunt they looked to be nothing more than jumbles of twigs bound together by filthy rags, mere breathing skeletons.

Soon the clearances were underway – the tumbling of the cottages by the landlords to turn the wee plots of tenant land into grazing pasture for cattle which was much more profitable. Unfortunates who were viciously evicted from their cottages for being incapable of paying the rents listlessly roamed the roads and byways only to languish and perish in the open air. Doomed souls lay alongside the already dead: mammies cradling their dead babes to their shriveled breasts, dying men clasping their dead wives and children, too weak to weep. Many a mouth was green-stained, having been stuffed with grass by a desperate hand in the vain hope of soothing the belly pains and staving off death.

Every day, Daddy, William and myself would ration out the dwindling supply of cabbage or onion that we had reaped from our meager plot of land and stowed in our cabin for safekeeping. The poor starving souls who traveled the roads would scrabble in whatever plot they came upon, not minding who 'twas who had planted it. Soon we were down to eating the crushed or rolled nettles. And though it like to broke his heart,

Daddy carried his beloved *bodhran* to a local merchant who took it in trade for a sack of oats which kept us alive for another month.

Those five years of starvation were a blur of pain and dismaying sights. We survived only because we were not victims of the clearances. We were able to keep our cabin which was only due to the decency of our landlord Mr. McConnell, God bless his soul. Himself had the rare kindly Anglo heart beating in his chest, and he didn't evict a one of his tenants though it brought him near to ruin. He was even after supplying us with the dearest bit of turf for our hearth during the coldest months. Thanks to him and the grace of God, the three of us made it 'til the gloriously fit potato crop of '50.

For a year 'twas like Paradise for we were back to eating our fill of fine healthy praties prepared in all the old divergent ways. Mostly just boiled with the bit of salt. But when Daddy earned a bit of money from the extra farm work, we could buy the buttermilk and sack of flour. Then we would grate the praties up with the onion, add the flour and buttermilk, and make the flat cakes of *boxty* all browned and fragrant. Or we'd mash the praties with the cabbage and the onion and the buttermilk and make the lovely *colcannon*.

Slowly we recovered our lost strength, and then weren't we just after being back on our feet and about our usual business when Daddy got the fever and within a wretched few days departed this earth. This was early in '52. I was but sixteen, whilst William was eighteen.

My brother and myself were sorely grieved. We surely loved our Daddy, and our future without his love and guidance seemed bleak indeed. But we drew solace from one another and 'twasn't long before William told me, "I'm not a one to scrabble in the earth all my life, digging praties and praying away the next blight. And I don't reckon you want that either, but that's all that's here for us. I've been after ruminating on it for some time and I've settled on a plan. I'll be going off to America as soon as I can earn my passage."

"Arrah," said I, stunned and hurt in equal measure. "How can you be after leaving me?"

"Just for a time little brother," he smiled and squeezed my shoulder. "Once I get myself settled in America and find a grand occupation, I'll save all the pay that I can and send it to you for passage so you can join me."

His amber eyes were after sparkling so with the hope that it leaked into my own self, and I saw the merit in his proposal. So 'twas that William loaned himself out to the aforementioned kindly landlord Mr. McConnell to work his vast acreage above and beyond to cover our rent whilst I tilled our little plot of praties and cabbages to keep ourselves fed. Thanks to Mr. McConnell's open-handedness, it took William only half a year to earn his passage money. And off he went across the sea. 'Twas a sad parting for us two, but we trusted 'twould be altogether good in the long run.

Many's the time since then I've pondered on the repercussions of William's plan and my participation in it. I've measured it from every angle, and I always deduce the same. It fashioned our vastly differing fates: valuable for him and calamitous for myself, albeit through no fault of my brother's.

Of course back then when the choice was made, young and uninformed as we were, neither one of us had any notion as to the ominous goings on in America that would lead to that damnable Civil War that destroyed me body and soul. At the time we were little more than boyos, and we trusted in the tales that claimed America was a place of endless bounty and freedom.

Arrah, what's done is done more's the pity, and brooding on it only makes the woeful heart all the more melancholy, as my scold of a wife Julia is always after telling me. And who's to say what would've become of myself had I stayed in

Ireland? And now 'tis neither here nor there, so that's all I will say about that.

At seventeen, I reckoned that traversing to this great country sounded like a right grand plan, so I was champing at the bit to go. But 'twould be more than another year before I finally joined William in Philadelphia, that great bustling city I called home until the war.

And what a lengthy, roundabout journey to get there! When William had arrived America, he'd had the devil of a time finding steady work, what with the odious 'Irish Need Not Apply' signs in many an establishment. After seven months of getting by at any odd job he could find, he finally landed employ laying ties for the railroad and was able to set the odd bit of money aside. After a few more months, he'd saved up enough to send me passage to Liverpool, the first stage of my journey. Thankful I was, for it suited my purposes. Liverpool was a place of easy employment and offered the cheapest passage rates to America.

Now Liverpool's long been a refuge for Irish looking for employment. Its bustling wharf is forever in need of laborers willing to break their backs for a pittance that they couldn't earn at home. However, 'tis a place one doesn't want to remain for any longer than necessary. 'Tis rife with murder and thievery and poverty. Many a poor bogtrotter has found himself mired there due to being swindled out of his savings by one of the multitudinous silver-tongued charlatans that prowl the quayside. Other wayfarers waste their time and money in the public houses and never do finish the journey they intended. I learned right quick that I had to keep a sharp eye about me at all times and stay clear of the drinking establishments.

By God's grace I was tall and strong, and I immediately found work on the docks hauling and loading the hefty bales and crates all the livelong day. Nights I slept in a scurvy, crammed boarding house teeming with every kind of vermin known to man and a few more besides.

It took me five months to save enough to book my passage. Beyond pleased I was as I traipsed to the booking office, dreaming of uniting with my brother six weeks hence.

So 'twas beyond dismayed I was when the clerk informed me they no longer offered passage to the port of Philadelphia, but only to New York.

"Arrah," said I, "Then how do I get there?"

"To Philadelphia?" the lummox inquired.

"Yes, to Philadelphia," I fairly spat at him.

"Once you're in New York, youse can book passage on a steamer."

"Another boat? But how much farther is that?"

"Couple hundred miles, I think."

"But how much will that cost?"

"Dunno." The *louser* shrugged his useless shoulders. "Don't work for them."

I turned and walked outside. Dispirited and stymied I was until I realized I had only the two choices. I could stay in Liverpool and work for the extra money I'd surely be needing for the additional fare though I knew not how much. This would delay my passage for I knew not how long because ship travel depended upon the state of the seas and the seasons.

My other choice was to buy my passage for New York this very day and upon my arrival in New York inquire as to the steamboat fares to Philadelphia. I would then write to William for advice and assistance.

Throwing caution to the wind, I returned to the booking office and purchased my ticket.

'Twas July of '54 when I boarded the *William Hitchcock* bound for New York. I was eighteen and nervous as a hare. The woeful plight on the coffin ships was common knowledge; half the ships travelling from Liverpool to New York were rife with the typhus fever, killing folks off like so many flies. But my fondest desire to be reunited with William overruled my hesitation.

For thirty-eight days I was buffeted in that ship's overloaded steerage as it shook and heaved over the waves. I feared 'twould be torn asunder at any moment leaving us all to perish in the sea. I was after suffering from the seasickness the entire time which was in truth a blessing, as I barely partook of the leathery dried meat, moldy bread, and foul water that served as our paltry victuals. 'Twas useful that I'd subsisted those Liverpool months in that filthy boarding house as it had equipped me for the putrid stink of close-packed, unwashed bodies. Arrah, but sure 'twas also after serving as a prelude to what lay ahead of me in just a few years in the Union Army, where nits were our constant companions and bathing was the rare summertime occurrence.

Anyways, 'twas mid-August when we arrived in New York harbor. As our ship slowly pulled into our berth in that bustling port, I could barely take in the vastness of the place, so much greater by far than Belfast or Liverpool. Excited as well as timorous, I stepped off that reeking ship, my sea-legs a quivering and nearly giving out from under me as they re-accustomed themselves to the firmness of land. I clutched my sack of belongings securely under my oxter - not for the trifling tattered garments it held, but for what I had wrapped within the clothing for safekeeping: Daddy's cherished books, which he had preserved throughout *An Gorta Mor*.

I freely admit to my trepidation as myself and my fellow passengers were disgorged upon the wharf with nary a fare-thee-well. Helpless as lambs were we set amidst wolves. No sooner had I set my legs upon dry land and taken note of the roiling mass of men and horses and carts and bales that surrounded me, than one of those preying wolves accosted me.

The scoundrel nearly knocked me over in his exuberance as he barked, "I see you're just off the ship and aren't you the lucky man that I'm the one that found you for I can get you anything you need. A job, a room, a nice dinner. I'm at your service."

His greedy eyes gleamed. 'Twas clear he viewed me as an easy mark. But my time in Liverpool had acquainted me with his type so I wasn't fooled at all. I made short shrift of him, pushing him aside and moving on into the crowd. I was accosted by numerous others as I tried to get the lay of the land and find my way to the steamship office. I dared not ask any of them for directions as I was sure they would waylay me by some deceitful trickery.

Eventually I found a fella loading a cart and asked him. He spoke in an odd parlance most difficult for me to follow and gave roundabout directions, but I finally located the place. As I feared, the fare was far more than the pittance I had left to me in my pocket. 'Twas necessary to find employ for to make up the difference. Meanwhile, I needed shelter and a bit of food. Then I would write to William and apprise him of my arrival in America.

Finding employ in New York was more difficult than it had been in Liverpool where every other fella was Irish. Here, they weren't so tolerant of us. I scoured that wharf offering my services to all I found, receiving one rebuff after another.

Finally, I entered a livery. Though I knew naught about horses, I offered to muck out the stables in trade for one sparse meal a day and a sleeping spot in the loft.

I wrote William and impatiently awaited his reply. Those ten days were endless. His reply was ecstatic. So glad was he that I had made the crossing safely and that we were now a scarce two hundred miles from each other.

More importantly, wrapped within the letter was half of the passage fare. William told me 'twas all he could spare for the nonce, but he would send more the next month.

Immediately, I wrote back thanking him for his generosity and informing him that I was on the lookout for any opportunity to make the odd bit of money to make up the difference.

Two more months elapsed before the two of us scrounged up the required amount of money. And so 'twas a lovely, bright October morning when I traipsed to the steamship passage office. I finally purchased a spot on a steamer that was to leave the following morning. I sent William a letter, telling him of my time of arrival three days hence.

As I rode down the coast and up the Delaware River to Philadelphia, I was a happy man, for I knew my very own brother was eagerly awaiting my arrival.

When my ship entered the port of Philadelphia and berthed amid the jumble of ships anchored at the vast wharf which was teeming with folks of all types, I fretted that I'd not be able to find my spindly brother in all of that mass of humanity. I needn't have worried. William, already grown accustomed to the throngs of that great metropolis, found myself scarcely a quarter hour after I set foot on land.

Whilst we embraced, we both shed tears of joy. I thanked God, His holy Mother, and all the saints for bringing me safely to my new home. My life as an American had begun. With my own grand brother once again by my side.

JULIA

Jesus Mary and Joseph, and what would I be after doing without my dearest brother Daniel? Himself's been with me through thick and thin, through a life of troubles, and I don't know where I'd be without him to lean on through all these years.

When we got to Belfast, we couldn't believe our eyes, so large 'twas with scores of byways and streets teeming with people and horses and carts. The clamor was near to deafening. We found our way to the market stalls where the lovely food smells got our bellies to grumbling. We chose carefully so as not to squander our passage money. We bought a great loaf of bread, a slab of smoked ham (which was a new pleasure for the two of us), and a jar of milk to wash it all down.

Down a alleyway, we found a quiet stoop to sit on and we set to filling our mewling bellies. 'Twas a grand feeling to be sure, 'specially having the bit of remains to stow in Daniel's sack. Then down the quay we went to the ticket office where Daniel bought the swiftest passage out on the *Windward*, leaving for Philadelphia in two days' time. We couldn't be after spending no more of our money that we'd surely be needing on our landing in America, so we slept the two nights huddled together on the odd doorstep. Thanks be to God it didn't rain hardly at all.

We boarded the ship with high hopes, us being young we didn't know no better. But more's the pity, we soon found our state woeful indeed. 'Twas a frightful six weeks journey across the ocean, the boat heaving and hawing the whole time and us folks all crowded in below decks like so many pigs in a pen. For that's what we smelled like. The foul stink of our dirty bodies and leaky slop pails made its way into every nook and cranny of that filthy ship.

Poor Daniel was after being gravely ill the whole time with the stomach heaving and then the belly flux. I fretted so that 'twas the deadly fever he was after suffering, but 'twas just the seasickness and the meager victuals which was beyond foul – being the salted dried beef, the moldy wormy bread, and the musty water. Thanks be to God, though wee, I've always been hale, and aside from the awful victuals I mostly suffered from fending off the rats what was big and bold as cats. Them vermin along with the nits was growing fat whilst we folks was after dwindling even more.

When we landed in Philadelphia, we could barely take in the bustling sight that lay afore us. Far greater than Belfast was this town, and the wharf seemed to go on and on along the river, and rising from it all was such an unholy din! The wharf was all a flurry of folk of every class and station hollering away, and with mules a-braying, and carts and horses and carriages all a-clattering and a-jostling, making such a racket as to wake the dead.

I was sore afeared to enter that swarming crowd, but Daniel though still wan was swiftly coming off the seasickness, and he took ahold of my hand and led me off the ship. Our legs, long unused to solid ground, were a-wobbly. I snuffled a few times to clear the stink of the ship from my nose only to be beset with new odors of horse dung and piss, tar, and rotting fish that hung about the wharf like a pall.

Daniel drew me through the crowd and into a alleyway. He said we could spare only a few pennies on food for we needed to secure shelter. After buying the cheapest loaf of bread – it must've been nigh on a week old for 'twas nearly hard enough to break our teeth -- we tramped up and down the alleyways 'til we found a boarding house 'twasn't all full up. 'Twas shabby indeed, and the drafty room we was allotted had just the one grimy cot, a wee rickety table with a washbasin and ewer, and a candle. But the owner – a old woman with a scabby face, a sour odor, and who talked through her nose in that odd American way – was more than happy to settle on the pittance left to us in Daniel's pocket for the first month's lodging. And as ourselves looked to be the filthy beggars and we'd had our fill of living in ditches and doorways, I thanked the Blessed Virgin that we'd found this humble shelter to keep us out the weather.

The first thing I done was check the cot for bedbugs. I found a dozen or so and burnt them one by one in the candle flame. Our nits was next, and they was on our heads, in our oxters and nether regions, as well as in our clothes. If I'd a had a pair of shears, I'd a cut our hair clean to the scalp. Luckily, I did have Ma's nit comb that I took out her pocket after she died. We begun by combing the nits from one another's hair and burning them nasty things in the candle flame. 'Twas a painful business getting through all them matted hair snarls and snags, and many a hank of hair come out in the process.

Next, we needed a good wash. I'd bought a cake of lye soap at the market back in Belfast, so first we took turns scrubbing ourselves from head to toe. The lye burnt my throbbing pate something fierce, but 'twas nothing for it. Whilst I scrubbed myself, Daniel picked and burnt the nits from my clothes. Then, whilst he washed, I did likewise for him. Our feet was so black and fouled we had to leave off getting them truly clean. For modesty's sake, we wrapped our bathed naked selves in the none too clean linens from the cot so's I could scrub our reeking, tattered clothes, which in truth were fit only for the burn pile.

Whilst we waited for them to dry, we ate a portion of the bread and made our plans to find work. Whilst I was fearful of venturing back out into that teeming city, Daniel was his usual sunny self, full of the big ideas. His rosiness made me hopeful.

Sure, 'twas a shame to don those tattered clothes once again for they gave us the look of shanty Irish, 'specially since we had no shoes to cover our grimy, hard-skinned feet. But leastways our garments were clean and free of the tormenting nits.

Then we two went searching for work. In spite of our raggedy attire, we stood tall and spoke mannerly to show what our true selves was after being. In Belfast we'd been told there was many an opportunity for work in Philadelphia. But 'twas after being a lie. We soon discovered they didn't take kindly to us Irishers. Myself and Daniel no sooner opened our gobs to speak than our Irishness came tumbling out and doors were slammed in our faces.

After a few days of boundless rebuffs, even my cheery brother was after fretting, for our pockets as well as our bellies was empty and in dire need of filling. We passed a grand inn alongside the harbor, and our dire state made us bold. We set our pride aside and went back to the alleyway in search of cast-off food. Just as we was picking through the bins, didn't a stout, elderly servant come round the pathway carrying a trash pail.

"Good lord Amighty," she clasped her hand to her great bosom. "What you think you doin?"

Astonied, I gawked at her. I'd never seen a darkie afore. Her skin was the color of strong tea, and her hair was short and crimped like black lamb's wool. Her eyes was black and sharp and her teeth strong and white.

"You're wastin' your time diggin' through that bin," she said. "There ain't nothin' worth your while in that trash."

Daniel, always a one to have his sharp wits about him, collected himself and smiled at her.

"We're only looking for the scrap of decent food. 'Tis hungry we are, ma'am. We've been looking high and low for work but to no avail."

"Work is what you're after?" She squinted at us as if doubting our intent.

"Yes, ma'am. My sister and myself are fit for any job whatsoever, nothing's too hard or too dirty for us to be doing. But 'til we find the work we'd be thankful for any food scraps youse could spare us."

Peering on us, her black eyes softened and she bid us follow her back up the path to the inn. She led us through the back door.

"Wipe them feet," she said pointing to the rug.

We did as we were bade, then followed her through a long hallway to the office of the innkeeper, an elderly man with bushy side whiskers and spectacles.

"Sorry to bother you sir," the darkie servant said. "I found these two young'uns rummagin' through the trash bins for food. They say they's desperate for work, and I didn't have the heart to turn them away."

The innkeeper looked us up and down. "Desperate indeed," he said, but with a kindly look in his watery blue eyes. "Are you two just off a ship?"

"We are that, sir," replied my brother. "I'm Daniel Regan and this here is my sister Julia. We are after needing work and we are willing and able to do anything."

"Anything is it?" He stood up and came around the front of his desk and his eyes skimmed over the both of us. "Do you have lodgings?"

"For the time being," replied my brother.

"When did you last eat?"

"Yesterday morn."

"When can you start work?"

"This very moment, sir," said my brother.

"I'm Anthony Lawford," the innkeeper said putting out his hand to my brother to shake, and Daniel complied though clearly astonied at the man's openness.

"It just so happens that I could use a scullery maid and an ostler." Mr. Lawford then gave us all the particulars. He said we would be after abiding right there on the premises! That way we would be close to hand.

"And this" he nodded to the darkie woman, "is Mrs. Hicks, my manager of domestic concerns. She will oversee you."

I was still astonied at seeing a darkie. At that time, I knew nothing about slavery, but I was soon to find out. Although there wasn't no slaves in Philadelphia -- only in the southern states -- Philadelphia was home to sundry dark folks who freely plied all kinds of trades. And on everyone's lips was the cause of Abolition and the looming conflict. Of course, 'twasn't 'til later that I was to learn all this. And then it made me altogether sad that dark folks so kind and able as Mrs. Hicks should be kept under the lash simply because of them being of a different sort.

Mrs. Hicks took us to the kitchen and instructed Cook to feed us. What a feast 'twas! Full of things we never ate afore: roast beef in gravy, peas, and to our especial delight – something she called a peach cobbler. We stuffed ourselves 'til nearly ill.

Once we'd filled our bellies, Mrs. Hicks led me up a narrow, bendy staircase and showed me to a wee room 'neath the eaves. To my delight, there was a iron bedstead with a plump, wool-filled mattress; a bureau on which set a kerosene lamp; and a washbasin and ewer with fresh towels and soap. She pointed to a key lying thereon.

"Be sure to lock your door chile, 'specially while sleepin' at night. For though we run a respectable establishment, we can't never be sure of the menfolk who lodge here. Though they be of means, some be real rakes, 'specially after they've had a drink or two."

Then she led me down the narrow hallway to a cupboard full-up with maid's frocks and caps and chemises and underdrawers and nightgowns and stockings and shoes, all from big to wee, all a bit worn but clean and fresh smelling.

"Take what you need, go to your room and get dressed. Be sure and pull all that hair up under your cap. There's pins and combs in the top bureau drawer, along with sundry other necessities." She looked down at my bare feet. "And make sure you wash them feet real good before you put them shoes and stockins on."

She left me to myself to go see to Daniel's keep. Alone in my room, the first thing I done was set on the bed for a bit to feel its lovely softness. Then, as I set to work freshening myself and scrubbing my feet, I murmured the fervent prayers of thanksgiving. I donned the lovely clean garments and the pinching shoes. Then I thought how proud Ma would be at my grand appearance, and I shed a tear.

Later, when I saw my brother, we compared our good fortunes. He grinned when he told me of his bed in the stable loft with its mattress full up with hay and horsehair. He was wearing fresh garments as well, though of a much coarser sort. And he sported hobnail boots in which he clomped about quite merrily.

So 'twas that we shed the shanty Irish look for to be altogether grand as respectable servants in a upright establishment. And though 'twas a blessing having the warm feet for once shod as we was, we was limping from the pinching and the blisters for days.

When we returned to the shabby boarding house to reclaim our meager belongings and give notice to the old landlady, the poor thing looked so woebegone at the loss of our keep that Daniel told her she needn't recompense us the remainder of the month's lodging fee. She blessed us heartily and wished us well.

'Twasn't long afore myself and Daniel settled into our new lives. Mr. Lawford was a lovely man who never stinted his servants on fresh food nor necessities for which we was beyond grateful as we knew what 'twas to suffer their lack. We ate plenteous hearty meals so our hollow cheeks and bellies soon filled out. We had the secure lodgings, the warm soft beds, and the clean clothes. The few pennies we was paid could buy the odd cap or bonnet or be set aside for the rainy day.

So we didn't mind the work at all, hard as 'twas. My hands and arms was always raw and chapped from scouring dishes and pots and pans all the livelong day. Mrs. Hicks, who was as kind as the day is long, gave me a big jar of her soothing balm which she said her Mama's people made for generations down south where they lived in the by-yoo. When I looked on her quizzically, she explained them are the swamps down in Louisiana. 'Twas a heavy concoction of tallow, beeswax, rosemary, lavender and lemon oil. I rubbed it in every night afore bed and 'twas a immediate comfort to my split knuckles and kept them from bleeding outright.

Meantime, Daniel cheerily toiled in the stables, as he come to love them horses mightily. He'd come in the kitchen every morning to greet me and then beg a bunch of carrots or some apples off old Cook -- who couldn't begrudge him anything -- for to give to the horses. He had a way with them animals, and they took to his gentle grooming and minded his every command like as if he was lord of the manor.

And so we gratefully served our rescuer Mr. Lawford for many a month. But as we was young and our days was long and our savings was meager, after that first year we became restive for a better life.

One day, I was after helping serve tea and coffee in the parlor -- the regular serving maid had took sick with the ague – and there I met a woman who changed our lives. She sat talking with another finely dressed lady sitting aside her, telling her that herself was in Philadelphia for the coming weeks to visit acquaintances and to see a surgeon about her rheumatism.

And I saw what the poor soul was after talking about when she took off her gloves to raise her teacup. Though not long in the tooth, she had the sorriest knobbly knuckles and crookedy fingers. So fiercely twisted was her hands that she had trouble holding the cup. My heart went out to her, though that good woman let not a whinge out of her on herself's behalf, but spoke as if her life was only after being nothing but sunshine and roses.

I was soon to find that this woman -- Mrs. Mortenson -- was a truly fine lady, gentle and kind though rich as a duchess. Anyways, as I was serving the drinks, I was keeping the one ear pinned on her talk -- for she had the loveliest of voices -- whilst trying not to tumble the teapot, the coffeepot, the sugar, or the cream.

"I do love Philadelphia," Mrs. Mortenson was after telling the lady sitting aside her. "My husband Arthur and I hail from here, so it's always a pleasure to return. We live in Gloucester City now, just across the river."

"Oh, I passed through there once," said the other finely dressed lady, who was stout and stern and full of the high airs. "Rather backward, isn't it?" she scoffed. "Just a dirty, dusty mill town, as I recall."

"I had mistakenly assumed that as well," Mrs. Mortenson smiled with the sweetness of a saint. "When Arthur informed me that we were relocating there so that he could take on the management of a textile mill, I was not at all pleased, let me tell you. But it's been seven years now, and I've grown to love it there. The people are really quite gracious."

"But the lack of culture!" the stern, self-important lady said with a sniff. "And how do you find reliable help in such a backwater town?"

"It is really a quite progressive town, and the people are the honest and hardworking sort, so I've never had trouble," Mrs. Mortenson smiled again. "In fact, when I return home, I will be posting a notice for a housemaid which I expect to fill quite satisfactorily. The faithful girl I've had since I moved there is marrying a local merchant and will be needed to assist her husband in his shop."

"What an ungrateful, selfish slattern to abandon a fine lady like you and run off and marry like that!" the stern lady harrumphed.

"Gretta is no slattern," said Mrs. Mortenson in a gentle but most firm voice. "Nor is she the least bit selfish. She's a lovely, loyal young lady, and I am very happy for her to have found such a good man for a husband, for she richly deserves him."

Just then I was bidden back into the kitchen by Alice, Cook's helper, but Mrs. Mortenson's words lingered in my head, and I wondered what 'twould be like to be after working for this grand and gracious lady away out across the river in a small town more like to what I was accustomed. This notion niggled at me all that livelong day.

That very evening, I sought out Daniel and told him what I'd heard and how I wondered should I be bold and approach Mrs. Mortenson to offer myself to be her housemaid whilst offering Daniel's services into the bargain. We nattered on about it a while, and I could see those cogs take to turning in his noggin. He was always a one to move on with the certainty of finding greener pastures.

"Though Mr. Lawford has indeed taken good care of us," he said, "'tis sure we'll not never be making much of ourselves here. So if Mrs. Mortenson be willing to take the both of us on, why not go gallivanting off across the river to a new place and see what's what?" Then he winked and grinned, which gave me some bit of courage.

And so, the very next evening after I'd rendered the kitchen spick and span, I hied to my room, scrubbed my face, rubbed Mrs. Hicks's balm into my hands for to make them presentable, and donned my best frock and apron. Then I returned to the kitchen where Alice was seeing to the evening duties, and I offered to take the tea up to Mrs. Mortenson's room. Alice smiled at me and said, "You are the answer to my prayers, Julia. My sore feet can't handle another trip up those stairs."

I took the tray on up. Jumpy as a cat I was, for I felt our very future rested on how I bespoke myself to Mrs. Mortenson. And being that she was so fine and learnt and myself was so rough and unlettered, I felt the distance between us to be vast indeed. But I recalled her loyal regard for her housemaid in shielding her from that harsh woman's rebukes, and that gave me pluck.

I needn't have fretted. That lovely lady listened in a most caring way as my words came out of me in a worried tumble: about how by chance I heard her speaking to the lady in the parlor and how I was keen to find better employment and that I would make a most able chambermaid and my brother who had a fine way with the horses was strong and nimble and up for any work, and that we was both looking to dwell in a quieter town. So, would herself be willing to take us back home with her?

Astonied was I at my own boldness which was not like me at all at all, but Mrs. Mortenson's smile encouraged me. Then she inquired, "Is your brother as hardworking and determined as you are?"

"That he is, and more so," I assured her.

"Can I meet him?"

"Sure and I can fetch himself this very moment, Ma'am." And off I scarpered to get him.

And being that Daniel was such a charming fella with his golden curls and his sea green eyes, he had only to smile (for his is one like the very angels themselves), to win Mrs. Mortenson over.

"Well Daniel," she offered, "My husband was recently remarking that we could use someone young and strong to deal with the heavier work around the place. Is that to your liking?"

"I'd be only too delighted, Mrs. Mortenson," Daniel grinned.

And so 'twas that we left the hurley-burley of Philadelphia and off we traipsed with Mrs. Mortenson across the river to Gloucester City. And though we was sad to bid goodbye to the motherly Mrs. Hicks and the kindly Mr. Lawford who cared for us in our time of need, we found Gloucester City to be quieter and much more to our liking.

Many's the reason our going turned out to be the best blessing. Our work was altogether pleasanter especially as Mr. Mortenson was as kindly as his good wife. Their house was a grand, three-storied place with a carriage house out the back where Daniel was quartered upstairs, while l had a cozy wee room on the third floor 'neath the eaves.

Most important, 'twasn't but two years afore I met James Lyons, the darling man who was to become my first husband. Now my James was a jewel of a man, so strong and gentle and good. And fine-looking as no man had a right to be --

he turned many a head with his brawn and his lovely dark looks. 'Twas at Sunday Mass that I first set eyes on him. I couldn't help it, himself was setting there in the pew directly in front of me. In truth, during Mass all of them mysterious Latin prayers betimes lull me into a kind of fog and I take to woolgathering, and so it happened this day that I found myself staring at the back of James's darling head, admiring his shiny black curls and then didn't my eyes take to roaming down his fine length of neck to his broad shoulders, and I was soon after pondering on things quite unholy, God forgive me.

And wasn't it my good fortune that my brother Daniel was acquainted with James from having traipsed into his smithy for nails and sundry tools. So after Mass, Daniel greeted him and introduced us. And I found the front of himself even more fetching than the back of himself. What with being a blacksmith and hefting them heavy tools all the livelong day, he was bigger than Daniel by a half. (Why is it we wee women are drawn to the big fellas?) He had the liveliest black eyes I'd ever seen, and the dimples to either side of his grin was deep enough to drown in.

Beyond tongue-tied I was as I felt the blood rushing and reddening my face. But James was charm itself, talking the leg off an iron pot he was as if he'd known me his whole life, while I shyly gazed at his handsome face.

For days (and nights) afterward, I pondered his fine-looking friendly self with a thrill of pleasure each time. Then the Sunday next, didn't he set himself directly aside me on our very pew at Mass! I couldn't keep my mind on none of the prayers as my eyes kept sliding sideways to catch a glimpse of that fine bucko.

Afterwards, I was beyond overjoyed when he accompanied me and Daniel all the way back to the Mortenson's. He spoke to me so gentle like and smiled so crinkly-eyed that my heart took to fluttering like a wee birdie in my breast. I feared that 'twas through silliness that I was pinning this vain hope of mine that James was rather taken with me. But 'twas clear to my brother as well, for as soon as we arrived at the Mortenson's front gate, Daniel said he had to look after one of the horses with a game leg, then winked and scarpered off to the carriage house.

That left myself alone with James. So timid was I that I daren't even look at his face for fear of him seeing my fiery cheeks.

"That's a lovely bonnet you've donned, Julia," James said to the top of my bowed head, "but 'tis your pretty face I'd rather be talking to."

I looked up and into them lively black eyes of his full of the tender mischief. He grinned which brought out those fetching dimples to either side of his lovely mouth. And that's when I lost my heart to James Lyons. For forever and a day.

We spent some time chattering and smiling on one another 'til it was clearly time to part. James peered on me with them beguiling black eyes of his and said, "'Tis been lovely talking with you, Julia. Would you be after taking it kindly if I was to come by next Sunday and walk you to Mass and back?"

His eyes was full of hope that sent my heart a-fluttering again, and I blushed hotly as I murmured, "Sure and that would be grand."

He smiled back at me in such a way that would melt a heart of granite. Then didn't he take my hand in his vast strong one, raise it to his soft lips and kiss it, sending a most delightful chill through my whole self.

And so our courtship began. We shared our stories. James told me of his boyhood in Sligo and how he'd come to America fleeing *An Gorta Mor* with his Ma and Pa. His poor Ma, heavy with child, died on the way over in that coffin ship rife with fever, and his heartbroken Pa lasted but a few years longer. So James was after having to make his way by his wits and his brawn from a tender age. Strong as a bull, he didn't have no lazy bone in his body, so he wasn't above toiling at any labor at all. When he was fourteen, he settled in to apprentice with a blacksmith. And when that blacksmith up and died without leaving no kin of his own, he left the smithy to James, who'd been working it ever since and doing a fine job of it.

Well, after three months of courting, didn't I have to tell dear Mrs. Mortenson of my plan to marry and leave her employ, as James told me I needn't go to work no more since I could settle down and tend to our own place.

She patted my hand and said, "Now that Gretta and you have both found fine husbands while in my service, it would be to my benefit to add in my advertising for a maid, that the position is most suitable to any young spinster with a strong desire to marry well as it attracts an array of desirable men for the choosing."

Then she gave me a little hug, and I knew she wasn't after begrudging me my happiness at all. And then didn't that gracious lady bestow on me the most lovely beribboned muslin gown in which to marry my darling man on August 10, 1855.

'Twas the happiest day of my life. I loved my James with all my heart. I knew I was the luckiest woman on earth to have a husband such as himself. A fine upstanding man was my James -- a fervent Catholic who was easy on the drink, never cursed nor said a bad word toward any living soul. He never missed a day's work, so

I hadn't a worry in my head for we always had the abundant food on the table and a cozy house to keep us safe.

When the war broke out in '61, I was sore afraid my James would feel honor bound to go off and fight and maybe get killed. And didn't he wrestle with that very idea, weighing his duty to country against that of family. But when his conscription seemed likely, didn't that kind Mr. Mortenson come to our aid, for he was ever after looking out for us. Being that he was an important businessman, he knew some officials. He pled on James's behalf, explaining that being as James was the only blacksmith for many a mile, he was needed at home. But more importantly, James was gifted beyond most blacksmiths as he was skillful at devising the odd apparatus and could render the war effort a useful service by forging sundry items for a mere pittance of their customary cost, which could then be easily ferried down the Delaware River. The officials was swayed and, needless to say, this arrangement pleased all concerned.

In the ten delightful years we shared together, James gave me five lovely babies, all different in looks and manner. Our first one, Johnny, was the spit of his Pa in every way. He was obedient and gentle, fun-loving and kind, and I was forever trying not to show him favor over the others.

Next came our Franky, who has always been my fair-haired *spalpeen* who is forever into the mischief, causing me the worries and the headaches. But he has a grin on him like his Pa's to melt the coldest heart, so's I could never stay cross with him for long.

Our Mary is as solemn as a nun and rather plain, but full of caring tenderness toward every living creature. She'd cry each time she was after finding a dead mouse or birdie. God blessed her with a lovely singing voice of which she is rightly proud.

Our Kate is speckled from head to toe like as if sprinkled with the cinnamon powder, and so cheery and loving with not a worry ever troubling her golden-haired head. She was slower than my other babies at the walking and the talking, so I fear at times she be simple. Born all blue she was, and took a time to cry and pink up, so she likely didn't get the air she needed. And though I fret about her fate in this harsh world, I'd never be a one to begrudge Kate's constancy of joy.

Our last one, Jimmy, is black haired like his Pa but with my green eyes. He's beyond clever and quick with the ciphering. To be sure, that's

why he's got a noggin on him as big as a melon --
to hold those bounteous brains of his.

And though our babies was so unlike each
other, they got along with hardly a cross word or
tussle between them. We was a gladsome little
family.

Them ten years I had with my James was the
only steady time in my life. We two loved one
another beyond explaining and could read each
other's minds and hearts. And our romance never
dwindled, but only grew as we kept having the
babies. James provided for us all so well that I
had nary a worry to bother my head. God blessed
us with good health, so's I thanked Him every
day for giving me such a virtuous, hard-working
husband and hardy babies that thrived.

But I wonder was I grateful enough. For of a
sudden my darling James took sick, and in the
blink of an eye my blessed life went topsy-turvy.

SAMUEL

When my three-week furlough expired in the middle of October, William returned me to that dreadful place of suffering, Cuyler. He was sorely distressed at my bouts of melancholy and terror that I had exhibited during my sojourn with him, and he begged the surgeons to find a remedy. He wanted me returned to myself.

But that was never to be. Myself was gone – all the scattered broken bits of my mind and heart were buried with Ezra and those other fine men who died fighting alongside me. May the earth lie gently on them.

Even so, the surgeons detained me at Cuyler for a further two months only to conclude that I had a nervous disorder. This shamed me, and I told them I was never a one to be seized with the nervous strain before, that it was all on account of poor Ezra's brutal demise which broke something in my head and swamped it afresh with all the horrors I had seen and made me to be so bothered with the shakes and the terrors and the black melancholy.

So I asked them -- each new one that came to inspect me like as if I was a peculiarly entertaining creature in a freakshow to be gawped at – I asked them was there something they could be after doing to abolish the dreadful sights that were forever in my head all the livelong day and all the livelong night, something they could dose me with that would make me unremember all that I'd seen and done, to set me to rights again.

Each and every one of those surgeons looked on me with heartless eyes, shook their heads, and told me that what I needed was to cease my morbid wallowing and be a man. They proclaimed that I was craven and ungrateful. Couldn't I see that I was after being one of the fortunate ones, as I still had my eyes and ears and skull intact and all my limbs in mostly working order? All I needed to do was be a true and noble soldier, proud of my service, and all of my difficulties would cease. Then, without so much as a by your leave, they'd turn their attention to the poor fella in the next cot.

Those worthless *amadans* didn't tell me how to cease the nightmares that assailed me every night and then bled into my waking hours, that fostered my morbid fright and melancholy. And 'twas no wonder since everywhere I looked at Cuyler I beheld mangled, suffering men. Surrounded as I was by the war's ugly consequences, I remained immersed in the horrors of it and couldn't recall anything of my former life, my former self.

My broken wits and sundered heart would not let go of the horrifying sight of Ezra's mutilation and death, the warm spurt and iron smell of his sticky blood dripping all down my face; nor could I let go of the gore and shrieks and reeking filth at the hospital barn afterward. All those riven bodies, all that blood, all that agony and misery. These visions preyed on my mind without end, sending me into fits of terror when I lost all vision and hearing so that I trembled in a deep black pit. And then further disturbing recollections started coming back to me.

The aftermaths of Second Bull Run and Chancellorsville came forth from the darkest recesses of my mind where I had thrust them from my horror-stricken heart: torn men lying in the gory fields moaning and crying for their mammies alongside dead comrades and sundry body parts -- all strewn about like grisly refuse from a slaughterhouse. The stink of blood and rot and shite assailing the nose and burning the throat as we wove our way through the gore to salvage the living and try to identify the dead.

And then burying all that mess of what was once an assemblage of honorable men in mass graves without a proper prayer service or even a marker to dignify those men's sacrifice.

Then into my head would return the battles themselves: the terrible hiss and percussion of artillery shells followed by the spume of mud and blood and chunks of flesh that left gaps in our ranks where countless men the likes of Finnerty and Brady and Keffler and Muldoon and Hermann had been marching mere seconds before. Good men, all gone like red fog that drifts away leaving nothing but clouded memory in its wake.

The taste of fear, dank and sour in the back of the throat, coating the tongue. You'd try to spit it out, but 'twouldn't go -- just rendered the breath rank and then sunk deeper into your sinews until it flooded your entire body and then oozed out in an unending reek of sweat.

These recollections battered me night and day as vivid as reality, and the more I tried to banish them the more they reared up in my brain 'til I was utterly beyond myself. I no longer knew who or what I was. I wished only to be dead so I could be rid of all of the suffering torment that assailed me with no quarter.

As I sank deeper into melancholy and terror, I became too vexatious of a puzzle for the surgeons. Not wanting to admit to their failure to find a remedy, they found it beneficial to rid themselves of me.

'Twas just a few days before Christmas – although I barely noticed -- that I was loaded into a wagon and taken to Christian Street Hospital nearer to the center of Philadelphia. 'Twas where they sent us hopelessly deranged ones, as it tended specially to nervous disorders. Dr. Morehouse along with Dr. Keen examined me and queried me. They were more tolerant than the other doctors had been, more attentive in listening to my troubles, more kindly in their looks and demeanor.

After two days, they made their venerable pronouncement: I suffered from a true bodily affliction called "Irritable Heart" which meant that my raggedy nerves caused my heart to palpitate in an unnatural rhythm which then caused the tremors and the black silences that I was after suffering. They had lately categorized this disorder which didn't lay the blame squarely on my lack of courage, but on my excessive sensitivity to the brutality I had witnessed. Their job completed, they shunted me to yet another hospital on Filbert Street for treatment of my "Functional Cardiac Disorder," which is just another appellation for "Irritable Heart."

Regrettably, although the surgeons had finally put a name to my illness, it became as clear as horseflies on shite that nary a one of them knew how to mend me. They allotted me a cot in a ward occupied by like Functional Cardiac Disorder sufferers who twitched and screamed and sobbed and stared popeyed into space, their wits bestrewn hither, thither, and yon. The surgeons came once a day to thump my chest and ask the very same questions over and over. Their cure was to leave me to "bed rest" in the midst of screeching, tortured men.

I grew so weary of their shite that by the middle of January, I had had my fill. Whilst unable to think straight, yet I knew I couldn't be after staying another day in that prison full of screeching lunatics run by quacks who couldn't remedy a one of us shattered men.

One sunny, frigid morning, I slipped out the side door of Filbert Street Hospital and kept on going. I deserted. I'd always thought that was a cowardly thing to do, had always judged deserters as ignoble and weak. But after being pent up in sundry hospitals for six months like some distempered beast and feeling none the better for it, my viewpoint had undergone a momentous alteration. 'Twasn't my post nor the battlefield I was after fleeing, nor my obligation to my men. I was fleeing the ineptitude of the army surgeons. Far from remedying me, they were rendering me sicker by imprisoning me in that quagmire of affliction that only served to stoke my melancholy and terror.

And though I was sorely beside myself in despair, I wasn't so beyond the beyond that I hadn't planned things out before I traipsed out into the teeming streets of Philadelphia. I'd lived in that populous city for seven years before I'd gone off to war, and I knew that vast town and its environs like the back of my hand: Germantown, Manayunk, Leverington, Washington Square. I'd labored in all of those quarters. Likewise, I knew the railroad depots and the street railway, and I knew the ferries over to New Jersey, where I'd had many an occasion to travel for the odd job in the years before the war.

I knew all this, and since my foremost fear was bringing misfortune onto my brother for harboring a deserter, I had tallied out what few coins I had in my pocket to see how far they could take me. If it had been within my choosing, I would have crossed the Delaware River to New Jersey and over to Gloucester City to harbor with my friend Michael Killian, a man I'd known for many a year and who has stayed with me through all the joys and sorrows of life. That way, the army wouldn't have the foggiest notion where to pursue me.

More's the pity, I had no such choice as 'twas bitterly cold January and the river was frozen so 'twas no ferry. And as everyone knows, there is no bridge. So unless I skated across the river, Michael's dwelling may as well have been in Shanghai.

As troubling as 'twas, I knew 'twas only the one place I could find refuge – with William in Manayunk. But I would do it only if I could shield him and his family from being found housing a deserter. And though I reviled with all of my heart the deceiving of my own dear brother, the only way I could protect him was to tell him I was on furlough. That way, if the army came pounding at his blameless door looking for me, he would be open and eager to help them and be genuinely astounded when they informed him that I had deserted, and he wouldn't be held accountable.

Of course, I would have to keep my wits about me at all times and be ready to slip out the back of the house, because although I had lost all joy and held my life of little account, I nonetheless wasn't keen on the ignominy of getting my neck stretched in a noose. Having settled all of that in my mind, off I tramped to Manayunk, riding the street railway and walking by turns on my circuitous route.

Though I had tramped many an arduous mile whilst in the service, this journey was grueling as my lungs were straining in the bitter cold. I commenced to coughing and sputtering up gouts of blood. Distressing as 'twas, I was becoming accustomed to it.

The first attack had come on me just the winter before, whilst we were stationed at Stafford Court House in Virginia. This was right before Rappahannock Station when I was promoted to Sergeant. The quack army surgeon had said it was a bad case of the grippe, but I knew better. No one coughs up blood with the grippe, only the consumption brings that on. My Mammy died of consumption, so I knew what my lungs were about. Still, I tried to put it out of my mind.

And that was when I first perceived the galumphing of my heart and the enervating faintness. Yet in spite of my sorry state, I was a seasoned soldier lately christened with the sergeant's stripes. So I had fortified myself to push on through the worst butchery of the war: Chancellorsville and then Gettysburg. And I've already told the sorry tale of how those battles ended.

Anyway, by the time I arrived on William's doorstep on Cotton Street, I was after feeling poorly indeed what with the shakes and weakness and wheezing. When he opened the door and saw my pitiful self, he snatched me in out of the cold, clapped a blanket round me, set me in front of the fire, and gave me a cup of hot strong tea with the drop of whiskey. 'Twas lovely indeed and settled my cough right down.

Then Lydia handed me a steaming bowl of stew, thick with beef chunks and praties and carrots and peas and with an aroma rapturous enough to raise a dead man from his grave. Poorly as I was, I ate as I had not eaten in many a month, spooning that glorious stew into my gob until I nearly burst. 'Twas being away from the horrors of the hospital and in the bosom of my own dear family that made me to calm just enough to feel a bit more myself.

As it turned out, I didn't have to dissemble to my dear brother. With my sunken eyes and sallow skin and bony frame and raggedy cough, I was clearly in such a state of unwellness that William assumed I was on medical furlough and never inquired about why I had appeared on his doorstep. But he was sorely perplexed about how I had gotten there.

"What were those daft surgeons on about, sending you out into the bitter cold to fend for your own ailing self?" William's amber eyes brimmed fraternal concern tinged with outrage. "Why didn't they notify me to fetch you?"

"Arrah," I told him. "They're nothing but a gaggle of *amadans*, don't you know."

"And how long will you be after staying?"

"Two or three weeks of Lydia's fine cooking along with a drop now and again of that whiskey in my tea should make me grand again," I lied. I knew I would never be grand again.

"You're welcome to stay as long as you need to, Samuel," said Lydia as she patted my shoulder. "Nothing will make me happier than to fatten you up and put some color in your cheeks."

Such a gentle, nurturing woman is William's Lydia. Such a blessing of a wife. Not a heartscald like mine can be when she gets on her high horse.

I remained in my brother's home two weeks, keeping my wits sharp about me the entire time, observing the street, straining my ears for the sound of horses' hooves and knockings at the door, jumping at every noise. Nevertheless, it did me a world of good to be away from the misery of the hospital, partaking of Lydia's wholesome cooking, in the bosom of the loving household of my own dear brother.

But as my resultant steadiness of mind began to return, so did a deep shamefulness and fear.

Ailing as I was, I had recovered my wits enough to perceive the imprudence of my desertion. My only hope was to return to duty of my own accord and beg for leniency based upon my unsound body and mind.

So on the first of February, I requested my brother take me back to Filbert Street Hospital. Upon our arrival, I insisted he leave immediately and not assist me inside with my haversack. I told him 'twas because I didn't want to linger over our parting as 'twould only make us the more melancholy. Consequently, he never knew of my desertion, nor of my everlasting shame.

Since I'd returned of my own accord and humbly asked for clemency due to my broken mind and body, I wasn't tried for desertion. But I was stripped of my rank of sergeant, which stung most deeply. A week later, I was returned to duty as a lowly private once again.

And although I shamefacedly rejoined my company two months later -- after my consumption had becalmed itself -- 'twasn't another month before I was once again suffering from the heart hammerings, the fearful weakness, the chest pains, and the fainting spells that came upon me of a sudden. I was in such a poor state that they sent me to the General Hospital in Madison Indiana. The surgeons there proclaimed I had "Hypertrophy of heart," a fancy term for an overly large, weakened heart.

There I remained, resting among similarly suffering comrades, though most of the time I spent there is but a blur. I cannot recall a single friend nor surgeon's face, for my bouts of black melancholy held me in a perpetual brood. Yet in due course, away as I was from the sights and sounds of the battlefield, I managed to recover a portion of my strength and my wits.

Finally, in November of '64, I was honorably discharged after three years and two months of service. I had no reason to celebrate for I was a changed man altogether for the worse. During that short space of time the best parts of me were torn out and replaced with naught but relentless sorrow and regret.

JULIA

First 'twas my darling James that took the diphtheria. At the outset, I reckoned 'twas just a catarrh or a touch of the grippe, what with his gullet being raw and sore and his nose running like a spigot. Himself being such a strong and hale man, I wasn't overly troubled. But by the second day, he woke with a scorching fever and his neck all swolled up. I fretted 'twas the quince, and when he started fighting for breath, I sent Johnny to fetch the doctor.

But Dr. Pratt shook his head, gave me the doleful look. and told me there was nary a thing he could do. James's gullet was so swolled inside 'twas nearly closed up and shutting off his air, and since he had but an hour or two at most before he would pass on, all I could do was send for the priest.

I couldn't hardly take it in; I felt I was caught in a nightmare and prayed to God to make me wake. I think 'twas Dr. Pratt himself who fetched

Fr. O'Boyle, for I have no recollection of sending for him. I just set on the bed, clutching my darling James's hand, telling him how much I loved him whilst I listened to his breathing getting feebler and his lovely face turning bluish gray. Thanks be to God he was in a fog and past most of his suffering.

My poor James lasted just long enough to receive Extreme Unction, after which Father O'Boyle turned his sorrowful face to me.

"Sure Julia, your man is heading straight to Heaven for he was such a virtuous sort that any venial sin that might have stained his soul has been cleaned away with the holy oil and the prayers."

Father O'Boyle's words were a great comfort to me -- for I didn't like to think my James would spend even a fortnight in Purgatory – but they did nothing to lighten my grief which was the worst agony I'd ever had to bear. Even worse than losing my Ma and Pa.

The quickness of James's passing was crushing, what with himself being hale and hearty on the Monday and on the Thursday lying stone cold dead in the bed. My mind was sorely muddled, unable to reckon what to do next. If 'tweren't for Father O'Boyle and my beloved brother, I don't know what I would've done. Father O'Boyle sent for Daniel, who came quick as he could, and the two of them saw to the burying arrangements. 'Twas a blessing indeed as I was beyond the beyond with the weeping and the sorrow. I was barely aware of my own babies, poor things, suffering their own sorrow for their dear Pa whilst their Ma could not offer them needed comfort.

Sweet Jesus, didn't I barely get my James laid into the ground when wee Johnny, my best child who was but eight years old, came down with the diphtheria he'd caught from his Pa. And hadn't I fretted that very thing would happen, for Johnny who was ever after being overly fond of his Pa hadn't kept away from James's bedside the entire time he was sick. I'd find Johnny after wiping his Pa's forehead with the cooling rag or holding his hand, and I'd shoo him away lest he catch the contagion, but as soon as my back was turned, he'd be after sneaking right back.

So, the very day after James's burying, Johnny who'd been laid low with the grief, came down of a sudden fevered and having trouble with the breathing, and my heart flip-flopped in my chest as I feared the worst. I peered into his gullet and was chilled to my very bones when I found it all aflame, and -- Jesus have mercy -- shrouding the back of it was a frightful veil of rheum like a birth caul all gray and glistering.

Directly I sent for Dr. Pratt who pierced the caul and drew it aside so Johnny could breathe more freely. I sat up with my baby boy all night, never leaving his side, swabbing his fevered brow, watching his every breath as he slept. But, more's the pity, by the following morn his breathing had turned raggedy and he was after struggling again. Afeared, I peered into his gullet and I could see that the deadly caul was growed back and, even worse, his gullet was nearly swolled shut just like his Pa's.

Whilst I waited on the tenterhooks for Dr. Pratt to come, I watched my wee boyo gasping for every breath, his lips going blue and with the wild fear in his eyes, and my heart never hurt so much as it did then -- 'twas as if 'twere being squeezed in a vise. All the while, he gripped my hand and looked on me for the easing I didn't have no power to give, and the retelling of it pains me all over again. I clutched my best boyo to my heart, raising him up for to ease his breathing as I kissed his fevered brow. All the while I stormed heaven to let me keep my dearest baby with me, but 'twas not to be.

My poor sweet Johnny, himself being so like his Pa and far too good for this world of suffering and woe, smothered to death not five minutes afore Dr. Pratt arrived.

I rocked his small self and wept so at his loss that the tears drenched his dear face as well as my own. I cried a river of tears which would not abate even as my eyes swolled shut.

Unbeknownst to me, Dr. Pratt sent for my brother to come and take care of things, but I barely took notice of him as I clung to my dead baby boy. 'Twasn't 'til my little Johnny grew cold and stiff in my arms that I let Daniel gently take him from me and lay him down.

But I wouldn't let no one else wash his body, readying him for the shroud. As I bathed his wee self, I looked on him through a veil of tears, recollecting his birth and all of the joyous moments he'd given me and his Pa in his short eight years of life.

Once again, Daniel and Father O'Boyle saw to the burial. After the Requiem Mass, I couldn't bear to lay my baby boy into the cold ground as he was forever after being afraid of the dark. But seeing as we were putting him right aside his Pa, still fresh in the double grave, I felt a measure of comfort that he wouldn't be all alone down there in the damp darkness.

So 'twas within one dreadful week that the first loves of my life were forever gone from me. In my blackest grief I fairly screamed at God, "You've taken my two best ones!"

Then afrighted of my mortal sin, I scarpered to confession where Fr. O'Boyle assured me that grief can cause many an unnatural feeling, and then that goodly priest bestowed God's forgiveness and wiped my sorry soul clean.

After this double loss, I was never after being the same. 'Twas the pair of these battering blows that crushed my heart beyond mending for I've never reclaimed my former self. Some bit of hopeful tenderness slipped out of me and a sort of wary hardness crept in. To be too devoted to any living soul was only to court sorrow, and so I girded myself against feeling undue fondness toward anyone ever again.

Yet not all of my tender feelings left me. Bereft as I was, I had enough of my motherly wits about me to ponder the needs of the four babies left to me. Hence the fear reared up in me for their wellbeing, and I steeled myself and turned my attention away from my mourning and toward them ones that lived. I had to get them out the way from our pest house of sickness and death. So I asked my good brother, who by this time had a wife and a wee home of his own, to take my brood back to his place where his dear Moira could tend to them.

Whilst they were safely out the house, I commenced to scrubbing and airing and boiling the linens. It did me good to be toiling away as it turned my thoughts away from the dead and toward the living. All the while I scoured and scrubbed, I pondered on my living babies and I stormed heaven that they would be spared, and our dear Blessed Mother took pity and answered my prayers.

Grateful I was, and I dared not linger no more on my dreadful sorrow, for didn't I still have four darling babies left to me? And wasn't myself sound and hale to care for them? Besides, 'twas never my wont to brood on what can't be changed. For where would we be if we all did that? Life is a vale of woe, but we must put all them griefs and sorrows behind us, close the door on them, and forge ahead.

My babies was looking to me for their upkeep, so I pulled my wits together and took stock of my state. 'Twasn't as dismal as many a poor widow has had to face, for I had James's smithy which was worth a pretty penny. Daniel helped me for to find a buyer, and I sold it along with James's sundry tools, and the takings kept us going through that black year of '65 and the next. When the money run out in early '67, we had to leave our home. We was taken in by my good brother Daniel and his Moira, to whom I will forever be grateful.

SAMUEL

Last night I dreamt of Ezra. 'Twas the same nightmare I have most every night when I know he's going to get that Minie ball in the face, so I throw myself on top of him and hurl him to the ground in the vain hope of altering the tragic past. But that everlastingly cheerful final face of Ezra always evades my grasp and pops back up grinning and then bursts open all over again, spewing gore. I watch in horror as his body slumps to the ground, his face blasted away.

Since '63 when Ezra got killed and I broke inside, I've ruminated over and over on that damnable war. From every angle I've tried to comprehend its worth. And it always comes down to me asking myself what exactly was it we were fighting for?

I joined up in September of '61 when Lincoln called for volunteers. I was twenty-six years old, no callow youth, but my espoused country, my new home, hadn't yet offered me much in the way of employment. We Irishers were not wanted. For seven years, I traipsed all through the environs of Philadelphia and up and down the Delaware River seeking labor anywhere I could find it. I was lucky the odd times I found the better paying job as a stevedore or warehouse loader. Mostly I toiled at the lowly jobs no native born would take: tavern sweeper, privy mover, gravedigger, fish scaler, stable mucker, whilst earning barely a pittance into the bargain.

Consequently, I was lured by the army posters offering the steady abundant pay of thirteen dollars a month along with the promise of the dignity and honor of soldiering for the Union cause.

The drilling and training, though perpetual and tedious, was easy enough for a hale fella like myself used to any hard labor I could find. In naught but four months I was promoted to Corporal. I reckon that was partially due to myself being a steady fellow and following orders so smartly, but mostly due to my fine skills in reading and writing which set me apart from most of my comrades. I confess it did my pride some good to be promoted so swiftly, and as I hadn't seen any real fighting yet, I was after thinking that soldiering wasn't a bad profession, something I might even settle into permanently. Especially since I was meeting so many fine fellas, most especially the aforementioned Ezra Cummings.

We two, we befriended one another straight off. He hailed from Philadelphia too, but he was native born, his people having come from Scotland many generations back. Ezra was the steadiest man I've ever known. But he likewise had a sly humor and delighted in many a comical anecdote which made him an altogether grand companion.

Arrah, here's the thing that keeps haunting me and won't give me a moment's peace. Ezra was a steadfast Quaker, and as such, he never should have enlisted; hence, he never would have left the security of Philadelphia for the sniper fire that killed him on that damned Cemetery Hill.

Now, I've been acquainted with the Quakers since back before the war, as they've always been plentiful in Philadelphia where they were known for being zealous abolitionists. As a young fella, I'd often had cause to pass by their fine brick meeting house on Arch Street where they'd gather, dressed in their plain garb, and I'd give a passing thought to their peculiar ways. They call themselves Friends and are a mild-mannered people, some still abiding by the queer ancient speech of "thee" and "thou." Being stalwartly opposed to war, they refrained from enlisting in the Union cause, though sundry of them aided the effort by tending the wounded.

Well, this one day as Ezra and myself marched along blathering about naught in particular, he up and tells me that he's after being a Quaker! My man had never let on, and it nearly knocked me on my arse, so astounded was I. Before I could gather my wits enough to natter him about how, as being the likes of a Quaker, he could be soldiering, Ezra commenced to telling me his history.

He was brought up in the way of The Friends according to his parents' fervency. He expounded on the mysterious worship practices of his sect. Since they reject pagan ways, their meeting houses are unwrought of any ornamentation, with nary a statue nor even a plain cross as those are held to be idols. They hold no credence in rituals of any sort, including communion.

Most peculiar to me is that they have nary a priest nor a minister to render rules and dispense God's laws, nor even to preach! Equality is their byword, so whilst they sit in the meeting house silently pondering on God's ways, any member at all can just stand up and sermonize whenever the spirit moves him! Arrah, even women can preach, as all folks are considered to be on an equal footing.

Then Ezra got to the nub of what was after prickling him. He elucidated on how The Friends hold fast to their rudimentary belief in opposing the following: paganism, social class and rank systems, violence, and slavery. And these fundamental beliefs were after causing Ezra a moral dilemma as two of them were sorely conflicting his conscience.

"In enlisting, I had to cast aside beliefs to which I, as a fervent Friend, had always held fast," he said with a most pained look. "I would be forced to acknowledge rank, and I would have to take up arms in a violent conflict. Yet I felt those impediments paled in contrast to The Friends' credence I hold most dear above all others." Ezra peered at me, "Have you ever had occasion to discourse with a slave?"

"I can't say that I've had the like," I mumbled, rapt to hear more.

"No condition is more wretched to behold," he sighed. "As you know, we Friends have always been ardent abolitionists. Consequently, my family home has ever served as a waystation for runaway slaves. I grew up beholding men, women, and children huddled in terror in our root cellar. I would assist my mother in delivering food and water to the runaways. One of my earliest recollections of their tragic plight occurred when I was perhaps six years old."

Ezra's eyes here took on a shimmer as he commenced.

"A young Negress was sheltering with us. Though a mere child, I was nevertheless struck by the profound sorrow that emanated from her. When I handed her a cup of water, she sobbed most pitiably. Later, my mother and I brought her food, and she put forth her hand to caress my face. Her own face ran with tears as she told me, 'You be remindin' me of my own baby boy. My Henry he be just 'bout your size when the Massa done sold him away. Don't know where he be now.' And then that poor woman broke into sobs."

At this point in Ezra's story, I must have gawped in revulsion for Ezra paused and nodded before he grimly commenced.

"Though her words and demeanor greatly distressed me, I was too young to comprehend their import. I asked Mother to clarify, and she enlightened me on the dreadful truth. Envisaging poor Henry's plight, I wept and clung to Mother as she embraced me. In that very moment, I came to understand that human bondage is the supreme evil of mankind. As the years passed during which time I encountered myriad runaways, my certainty in the Abolitionist cause only intensified, especially when I beheld the barbarous mutilations inflicted by savage slave masters. Innumerable slaves' backs and legs were covered in tangles of loathsome scars exacted with the lash. Then there were the slaves whose faces were branded, whose ears or tongues had been clipped off or whose limbs ended in stumps betokening chopped off hands or feet – punishment for 'stealing' or trying to run away." Ezra turned to me.

"Many of the children were lighter complexioned than their mothers and had Anglo features - some could've easily passed for white – which betokened their begetting through barbarous compulsion of master or overseer." Ezra shook his head in revulsion. "What kind of man commits such an atrocity on a helpless woman?"

I could only shake my head in repugnance, for this was a sobering education.

"Thusly when the war broke out," Ezra continued, "I found myself faced with an ethical dilemma. Shall I follow the way of The Friends and remain a peaceful citizen aiding the occasional runaway slave in his or her dash for freedom? Or do I cast off a fundamental belief by taking up arms as the only sure way to abolish this barbarous evil of slavery for all time? I consulted the Bible for wisdom and ruminated vigilantly upon my choices. Whereupon my conscience instructed me that because slavery is an abomination to both natural and moral law, my taking up arms to procure absolute abolition is a higher calling than refraining from the war."

Well, I have to say that Ezra shamed me with that speech of his, for I hadn't given much thought to the plight of the slaves, having never had an occasion to see one. I'd joined up for the steady pay along with some vague notion of glory. But I have to say that his heartfelt righteousness did aid me in upholding belief in the Union cause as some higher calling as time wore on and the fighting grew ever more fierce.

Until Ezra died, that is. His parting shattered my belief in the rightness of our cause forevermore. For though I earnestly believe in God-given freedom for every man no matter his color or tribe, nothing could be worth the shedding of all that blood on both sides, most especially the blood of my man, the most righteous Ezra.

When I think back to a mere year before Ezra's demise in all that gore of Gettysburg - in the early summer of '62 - I was still my original unbroken self as were my comrades in arms. Our regiment was in high spirits since the sole battle we'd witnessed was Cross Keys where we were kept back of the action in reserve. We didn't have a true notion of battlefield horrors, so we were more like a gang of lads playing at war.

High-spirited tomfoolery ruled our free time, and during our incessant marches we could always rely on the antics of Ned McElwee to keep ourselves amused. Our man Ned enlivened many a tedious march. He was always after being such a comical fella. He loved to sing in his high, scratchy voice, and he'd regale us by inventing songs as we plodded along. Soon we'd all be after forgetting our blistered feet and weary limbs and pestering nits and sunburnt faces.

I remember one ditty in particular that always set us all to chortling. The best bits are not proper for polite company, but I'll provide a mild bit that went something like this:

> *Oh, how I adored Marie,*
> *Prettiest gal you ever done see,*
> *Raven hair and ruby lips,*
> *Plump white bosom and swaying hips.*
> *With her sweet and dimpled smile,*
> *She did all the boys beguile,*
> *'Cept when one would start to leer,*
> *She'd turn on him like a mama bear.*
> *'Til one time a man named Jay,*
> *Found it was his lucky day,*
> *Marie did grab him by the hand,*
> *Led him to the Promised Land.*

And on and on the song went, getting bawdier each time we asked Ned to commence singing it.

Himself was also after being a fine storyteller – if he'd lived in Ireland, he'd surely have been the town *seanchaidhe*. Oftentimes of an evening, whilst we were all after being restless in that muddy and frigid winter encampment in Falmouth Virginia, Ned would regale us with reminiscences of his patriot granddaddy who'd crossed the Delaware with Washington and distinguished himself at those grand battles of Trenton and Princeton.

It gladdened my Irish heart to listen to how the patriots thumped those English devils but good, ultimately throwing off the heavy yoke of their tyranny. And it offered me hope that one day my own native countrymen, proud descendants of the likes of Brian Boru and Finn MacCool, would be able to do the same (a hope that I steadfastly cling to to this very day).

That first year of our soldiering was all marching and being held in reserve. But then in August of '62, our innocence suddenly vanished when we engaged in our first serious battle at Second Bull Run.

Now I know lots of folks accept as true the adage that the Irish love nothing more than to be in a good fight. And 'tis true up to a point. We are a passionate, wild lot, easily incensed at injustice of any sort as well as driven to prodigious sympathetic defense of any suffering man or creature. The thing is, we Irish bear our robust emotions on the very underside of our hides from whence they are bound to be bruised and leak out at the least provocation.

And many's the time I've seen two Irishmen bashing one another's faces to bloody pulps in the boxing matches as well as in the public houses, mainly after imbibing in too much drink. But, we Irishers aren't all after enjoying pummeling one another in the *gob* or getting our noses wrecked. That's especially true of yours truly. Daddy was a peaceable gentleman who taught my brother and myself that it took more of a man to walk away from a fight than to give in to one. And I've steadfastly followed that sage advice, which has saved me many a time from a savage throttling and a crookedy snout.

So, due to my proper upbringing and amiable nature, battle was not something I was keen to face, though I never considered shirking my duty. Then along came Second Bull Run, and 'twas an eye-opener all right. 'Twas my first full-out battle and I was sorely afraid, mostly because all was utter mayhem. We couldn't recognize friend from foe due to the sulfurous smoke that seared our eyes and gullets and the horrific din that blasted our ears. We just marched forward, fired our rifles straight ahead and hoped to God it was rebels we were after shooting. After a time, my fear gave way to a kind of mindless fog, so I can't recall particulars.

But after 'twas over and we beheld the gruesome consequences – the blood and gore and stink of scores of butchered men – 'twas then myself and a whole lot of others began to suffer misgivings about the army's discernment of glory. Poor peaceable Ezra was shaken to the core in spite of his steadfast belief in the righteousness of our cause, and every one of us was beyond sickened at the carnage.

This dawning trepidation of the true butchery of battle weighed heavily upon us even as we settled into our dismal winter encampment in Falmouth Virginia. 'Twas there in December of '62 that I took my first Minie ball when some rebel scouts blundered into our encampment. We skirmished, and a ball broke my right pointer finger that's crookedy and useless to this day. I paid a visit to Doc Gunkle, our regimental surgeon, who stitched and splinted it and ordered me to go easy on it for a month. More's the pity, it never did straighten out, but curled like a claw into my palm, which causes many a problem with the grasping of things.

The worst of 'twas that to my great misfortune I was born a *ciotog*, so 'twas my *left* hand and pointer finger that I needed to be able to grasp and pull the trigger. Had I been right-handed, my injury would have rendered me unfit for duty and 'twould have saved my lungs from catching the consumption that's been eating them away ever since. But as 'twas my lesser used hand that was damaged, 'twas considered just a minor wound.

'Twas our great misfortune that December of '62 through January of '63 was a particularly frigid winter season with the sheets of freezing rain and the resultant mud making our lives a song of woe. As if encampment wasn't enough of a trial, that shitebrain General Burnside sent us marching off in that hellacious weather on an utterly ill-planned expedition to cross the Rappahannock and capture Richmond. Such an abysmal failure was it that it came to be known as the Mud March, and it ruined my hale self forever.

'Twas on January twentieth of '63 that we set out in that rainy, frigid weather that had dogged us for the past month. For five endless days and nights we marched and slept in the icy rain, our clothes so sodden and the wind so vicious I thought we'd all perish from the cold. The roads had turned to quagmires and everything bogged down: horses, mules, wagons, cannons. And we men did, too. At every miserable step of our frozen feet the mud sucked at our sopping brogans. The wretched horses and mules were so worn to exhaustion that many simply died in their traces, becoming odious obstacles for ourselves to navigate.

Yet we soldiers kept on going, as miserable as we were, with no respite in the nighttime for no shelter was to be had. We huddled together like shivering pups trying to keep warm under our sodden blankets, but to little relief. We slogged through the ceaseless icy rain that froze us to our very marrow whilst we cursed every last one of those whoresons who'd had a hand in the bungling of it.

On the third day of agonizing cold and wet, that great *amadan* Burnside -- who should have been court-martialed for his heartless and deadly incompetence at Fredericksburg – committed another gross miscalculation. He doled out liquor to ease the griping of the men. Unsurprisingly, that just made the dejected soldiers ornerier, and they started picking fights with one another. What a sorry mess! How we survived nearly intact is nothing short of a miracle, but 'twas then the cold settled in my lungs bringing on the catarrh and the consumption. Yet in spite of my fever chills, wheezing, and coughing, I soldiered on through Rappahannock Station, gaining my sergeant stripe for my tenacity.

As awful as that Mud March was for my comrades and myself, what lay in store was far worse. The slaughter and humiliation of Chancellorsville was what truly opened our eyes to the army's deadly ineptitude. Even now, nigh on eleven years past, it angers and sorely pains me to recall that calamity.

'Twas the second of May of '63 when General Howard's grievous incompetence situated my company directly within a death trap. Right on up 'til Chancellorsville, we'd trusted him, as he'd fought admirably at Fair Oaks the year before, even losing his right arm in that engagement. More fools we, for at Chancellorsville it seemed that Howard had left his wits back at Fair Oaks along with his amputated arm. Arrah, that shitebrain positioned us in an exposed curve in the line and ordered us to dig rifle pits and settle in. Immediately, General Hooker perceived this was an unsound position, that we would be outflanked. Dutifully, he warned Howard to move us, but that great *amadan* discounted the warning and abandoned us there.

And by God, just as Hooker foretold, Stonewall's rebels came aswarming at us from every which way, shrieking their bone-chilling yell 'twould put any wailing *banshee* to shame. We fought our utmost to repulse those devils, but being vastly outnumbered in our tenuous position, we suffered such horrific casualties that we were obliged to retreat like whupped curs, leaving scores of dead and wounded.

Later, we gathered them up. A sorrier duty I never knew. Back in Ireland, I'd seen many a famished body lying dead along the roads and fields, and I knew the death stench all too well. Yet this was something else entirely for we had partaken in this butchery. So much blood, the iron tang of it hung in the air like a grisly pall. Some of the dead were blasted beyond description, just gory tatters of flesh scattered hither, thither, and yon. As for the living, the appalling wounds to faces, bellies and limbs would never mend to their former usefulness and beauty. All of this savagery imposed on men whom I had marched with just hours before.

Above all, the dawning that I had taken part in this carnage, had inflicted it on other men. For a portion of these riven bodies were secesh.

Afterwards, we courageous men of the Eleventh Corps suffered further torment regarding the rightness of our retreat. Though 'twas necessitated by that whoreson Howard's reckless orders, we were forevermore falsely branded as craven turn-tails when nothing could be further from the truth of it.

Heartsore though we were, Ezra and myself sustained one another, buoying each other's spirits through all of our travails. As close as brothers we became, and the both of us survived for precisely two months. Until Gettysburg.

On that first sweltering day of July, we marched for miles through the soupy air, our throats ragged and raw from thirst and dust. Reeling from the heat, we sweat clear through our linen shirts and woolen coats 'til they were sodden enough to wring. On up the Taneytown Road to the town of Gettysburg we trudged, then onto the high ground of the cemetery where we stopped and awaited our orders.

Much to our revulsion, we were still under that *amadan* General Howard's command, so we were wary of what further deadly mismanagement was to come. Finally, Colonel Coster, who headed our First Brigade and whom I trusted, came and gathered myself and a couple of other regimental sergeants together to inform us that the rebels were fast gaining control of the town from the north, and so he was going to lead our companies up Baltimore Street into the very center of that cursed place to try to clear them out.

So, off we went at the double quick, all the way up Baltimore Street about a mile, 'til we reached the square at the very center of town. Coster led my company to the railroad depot two blocks north and ordered me to hold the position against the rebs whom I could see advancing just beyond the other side of the tracks. Hastily, I positioned my men. The two opposing army lines – ours of uniform blue and theirs of raggedy gray or butternut or simple homespun – peered at one another across the fifty-foot divide with resolute hostility.

Meantime, Coster led the others a block to the east over to a brickyard. 'Twasn't long before all hell broke loose. The secesh devils began bombarding us all along our line with artillery and rifle fire. 'Twas while I was pondering my next move when I saw Coster and his men hightailing it back to the square, and he signaled me to follow. I ordered my men to withdraw back down Baltimore Street, and we covered Coster's flank from the rebel sharpshooters who granted us no quarter.

We withdrew all that long mile south and up through an orchard to the high ground of Cemetery Hill from whence we had started. Scarcely had we returned when our regiment commander Captain Kelly informed us he was going to lead us back along Baltimore street to search and secure the buildings as far north as possible.

Off we went, and it didn't take us long to take possession of several houses and a hotel to either side of the road. But before we could advance further, the rebels began firing from the tannery just beyond. Those devils drove us back, and we took cover inside a house and engaged them until nightfall, neither side giving an inch.

Beyond exhausted, we sank into fretful slumber. Just before dawn, Ezra and myself and a few of the others were ordered to return to our regiment on Cemetery Hill. There, we joined our courageous comrades of the Eleventh Corps and held that high ground for another two days. We suffered withering sniper fire the entire time, but our steadfastness in holding that vital position enabled the Union to claim its first decisive victory of the war.

More's the pity, neither Ezra nor I were able to witness that victory on the third day of that appalling battle, for 'twas on the second day all went awry for us. 'Twas nearly dusk when Ezra's face was burst wide open by that damned rebel ball. I'd yet to comprehend the loss when we were ordered to rush out the cemetery gate to defend Wiedrich's battery which sat just on the other side of the pike, defending our position.

In a daze, I raced with my comrades on the double quick through that arched gate and across the road just in time to face the onslaught of rushing, howling Louisiana Tigers -- fiends who were acknowledged by all to be the fiercest and wildest of all the rebel regiments. They were hellbent on overtaking our cannons and turning them round to fire against us. This would have surely doomed our vital position on the high ground and won the entire battle for them.

Just as those devils clambered up out the dark of the sunken path and over that rise bellowing their bloodcurdling rebel yell, I felt a fierce tug and then a piercing burn in my left arm, above the elbow. I was too engaged in defending myself to take much notice, for by now we were face to face with those rebel foes and 'twas fists and bayonets doing the dirty work. Barbaric 'twas.

I can never forget the feel of the bayonet as I thrust it into one rebel's belly, through flesh and sinew and guts, then the terrible turning to and fro to be sure of mortal injury, and the sliding back out. Though 'twas dark, he was so close I could smell his rank breath and make out his aggrieved eyes which have never left my mind. How they opened wide in agony then fogged over as he slumped to the ground at my feet spurting his life blood, drenching my trousers and brogans.

Amid such brutality, we ultimately sent those cursed wild Tigers scarpering back down the hill, thereby preserving our crucial cannons and our vital position on the high ground. 'Twas in that moment of relieved triumph when I felt the throbbing ache in my arm and beheld the ragged hole in my sleeve afoul with blood, dripping like a spigot onto the ground.

I didn't know it then, but my fighting days were well and truly over.

'Twas four months later while enduring the misery of Cuyler when I read in the newspaper that President Lincoln travelled to Gettysburg and stood in that cemetery near the very spot where Ezra was slain. Lincoln offered a few edifying words expounding just how all of our suffering and dying was for a lofty purpose. He claimed that our sacrifice was a holy endeavor on account of it being to secure our countrymen's full liberty by freeing the slaves. And whilst he mouthed Ezra's abolitionist sentiments, he failed to soothe my mourning over Ezra's loss.

I allow that those darkie slaves suffered an unjust, woeful lot in life what with being bought and sold and beaten like beasts. Yet I cannot accept that Ezra's dear life should have been bartered to end that two-hundred-year-old devilish institution which would ultimately have crumbled of its own demerits.

Nor should the likes of Finnerty, Brady, Keffler, Muldoon, and Hermann been mown down in their prime. So many good men gone. And more's the pity, 'twas only six days following Lincoln's speech at Gettysburg where he extoled us to the heavens, when that jolly, comical Ned McElwee along with the brainy Gilroy and the timorous Curry and a few other fine fellas were captured at Missionary Ridge. They were marched off to that infamous Andersonville Prison in Georgia where those three good men sickened and starved to death along with thousands of their comrades amid the brutality and the filth.

Nor should I have lost my wits and my vigor to end the curse of slavery in this country, since its implementation and shame had naught to do with me. Rather, I should have returned to Ireland and fought to free my own people from the shackles of brutal English law which has stripped them of their rights. Little more than slaves themselves, my people have never been more than an Anglo plantation owner's whim away from eviction and death.

As for the rebels I saw, most of them were such a sorry lot being all scrawny and tattered looking. Underfed, most didn't even wear uniforms, just raggedy old farm clothes, and only the fortunate ones had brogans. Now, if they couldn't feed nor even dress themselves properly, how could they be after keeping slaves?

No, those rebel farm boys were duped into fighting and dying same as we Union boys were. They were tricked by the powerful plantation owners who needed to preserve slavery to keep their massive fortunes intact. Of course, the politicians were of that selfsame ilk, intent on furthering the southern economy. So they fired up those rebel boys with the notion that we Union boys were invading their land, treading on their "states' rights."

Worse still, they stoked the men with the fear that already existed among all laborers North and South: if the slaves were freed, they would take the meanest jobs the lower classes had subsisted on; they would steal the common laborer's very livelihood. And in the southern states, those liberated slaves would do the intolerable -- they would elbow those poor white farm boys aside and climb a rung or two higher.

When those arguments didn't provide them adequate volunteers, the Confederates enacted conscription, which worked so well that the Union followed suit. Of course, both North and South were beholden to the rich folks, so on both sides a man could be exempted by paying a $300 fee or by paying some poor fella to take his place. For middling and poor folks there was no choice but to fight one another.

Eleven years on, I've come to comprehend the sorry truth. We were all – Union and rebel soldier alike -- merely pawns of the rich and powerful. Hardworking, decent men, we were hoodwinked or obliged into killing one another with inhuman ferocity. Such an intolerable waste.

Looking back, I tremble to think how many of those poor southern lads I killed or maimed. Those fellas like me, who held no investment in slavery at all, who had joined a cause beyond their ken and then were simply trying to stay alive.

JULIA

As I said afore, when the money from the sale of James's smithy run out, myself and my four babies was taken in by my brother. Now, Daniel was already after being burdened with the wife and three babies of his own, so I knew we was adding a weighty load onto his poor shoulders, what with our five added mouths to feed.

But even amidst our trouble we was all after being blessed, for over the years that kindest of men Mr. Mortenson had grasped my brother's cleverness and had raised him from his humble position as workhand all the way to being manager of his estate. So's Daniel was after earning a tidy sum. That made it easier for me to accept his hospitality with good grace, and I thanked the good Lord each and every day that I had such a kindly brother as he.

His wife Moira was lovely about it, never begrudged me a thing, never grumbled, nor gave me no black look of reproach. In gratitude, I went about cleaning and tidying with a glad heart, taking on the coarsest jobs myself, such as emptying the chamber pots and plucking the chickens. Our babies all lived together in a house full of love which rendered my grief less burdensome.

During my ten years married to James, I'd seen Mrs. Mortenson galivanting less and less around town. Poor thing, her rheumatism was taking its toll, crippling her legs so's she couldn't hardly walk. This made me altogether sad as herself had made a life of kindness. In spite of her affliction, she'd paid her respects at my James's funeral and sent me a generous basket of victuals.

Her lovely self had been preying on my mind, so's I called on her one day whilst out on an errand to see how she was keeping. She was only too happy to see me and invited me in for a cup of tea. Her poor fingers was so gnarled up, she had to lift the teacup with her palms, and even then was after having a terrible time of it. My heart hurt awful for her.

Never a one to make a song of her sufferings, she waived away her misfortune to inquire after my doings.

"And did you fashion that lovely dress you're wearing?" asked she, nodding at my frock.

'Twas my Sunday one, emerald green worsted which I'd trimmed with the odd bit of satin and lace and for which I was most proud as the cut and color flattered my trim figure and brought out the green of my eyes.

"Sure, and I thank youse. I've always been after making all of my own clothes and my children's as well."

"You were always gifted with the needle. Your mending was a wonder, invisible to the eye."

"'Twas a skill born of need, being as I was always a one to be in humble circumstances."

"A talent nonetheless." She peered at me. "I have a proposal for you, Julia. Please feel free to decline my offer, but would you consider fashioning several gowns for me? I would recompense you generously, of course. These days it's rather difficult for me to traverse to the milliner's shop to get fitted, and she's so busy I can't impose on her to come here. Consequently, my frocks have grown rather tattered."

"I'd be only too delighted," said I with all truthfulness, for to aid this kind lady was my fondest hope.

"That's perfectly wonderful!" she smiled. "I trust you to choose the appropriate fabrics and trimmings. You know my tastes and color choices. I will provide you with a letter instructing Mrs. Warren that your purchases should be billed to my account. When can you begin?"

"This very day, Mrs. Mortenson. If youse can be after giving me an old frock, I can take it home with me, dismantle it, and use it to pattern the new one. Then I'll bring it back here so youse will need only to stand for the final alterations."

The arrangement was a blessing for the both of us. That dear woman was after being so pleased with her garments that she praised me to the heavens every chance she got so that a number of her acquaintances asked me to fashion frocks for themselves as well. Thanks be to God I was finally able to give Moira money for to help with the food and household necessities of which she was truly grateful.

Though myself and my brood was being well looked after, I was still after missing my darling James something terrible. And our little lost Johnny came to my mind at all times of the day, as he does even now all these years later. Recollecting his fetching ways and his sunny smile would bring many a tear to my eye. But I took comfort in the four hale and lovely children God in his mercy had spared.

Every night, I gathered my brood about me in the wee, cozy room off Daniel's kitchen, and we'd kneel by the big bed and say a *Ar nAthair* and a *Se do Bheatha a Mhuire*. And, as I knew God's ear gives a particular listen to the prayers of innocent children, I'd lead them in prayer for their Pa and brother, and then for their Uncle Daniel and Aunt Moira, and Mr. and Mrs. Mortenson, thanking God for their many kindnesses.

Once that was ended, I'd gather them all to me in the bed like a mammy bitch with her pups. As soon as I was after hearing their soft snoring, I'd let myself ruminate on things. Sometimes I silently wept for what was lost to me, but mostly I turned my thoughts to gratitude for what I had.

And so it went for most of a year. Until the autumn of '67 when I met Samuel. And my life took another big turn.

SAMUEL

The consumption is gnawing my lungs away. They're naught but a pair of burning, worn out bellows rent with holes. 'Tis been four months since I've been able to earn any pay, and I'm still after trying to get the army to pay me the pension due me. Jesus Mary and Joseph, it's been two years since I filed, and it's been a right battle the entire way. I thought I was all done with battling in '64, but here I am ten years later still fighting.

The long and the short of 'tis: my left arm is feeble; my right hand is crippled; and my raggedy lungs are wracked with coughing that brings up the bloody catarrh and renders me unable to draw in sufficient air.

Worse still, I've yet to regain the soundness of my own mind, still melancholy and going all astray in the wits at the odd time with the galumphing of the Irritable Heart and the blinding and deafening fainting spells. For that there's no cure aside from the pleasant numbing of the whiskey bottle. But as the drink is far too dear for our empty pockets, suffer I must.

Presently, the Government allows that I have the two bullet wounds, for the veracity of the scars can't be denied. The ball I took at Gettysburg tore through the flesh of my left arm which healed up well enough, but it rendered the muscles feeble which hinders hard labor. The first ball I took in the finger during that skirmish at Falmouth in December of '62 never mended rightly in spite of good Doc Gunkle's ministrations, and to this very day my finger won't flex. 'Tis all crookedy and knobbly and bent like a claw because at the base where it meets the palm it's all webbed with thick, scarred skin. I sometimes think 'twould be better to lop it off as it interferes with any sort of grasping tasks.

Consequent to these injuries, the government allows me disability of one-fourth degree – two dollars a month. But they won't take into account my worst debilitation which is the consumption, because they claim they are not accountable for it even though it is a direct consequence of that hellacious Mud March that we were forced to endure in January of '63.

And though I was robust and hale before that abysmal march with nary a sniffle, the coughing commenced directly afterwards, and by early

Spring I was spuming up gouts of blood. Arrah, that gave me the jitters as it brought back recollections of Mammy and her bloody kerchiefs, and I surmised myself was after having the consumption.

By that time, good Doc Gunkle had been replaced by a new regimental surgeon by the name of Crump who didn't know his arse from his noggin, and he proclaimed I was just after having the grippe. Wanting to believe, I took that *amadan*'s judgment to heart and in spite of my ailing, I kept so well to my duties that at the end of April I was promoted to Sergeant.

Forgive me if I've told all this before. 'Tis hard to keep my thoughts going in an orderly fashion, for the memories come back to me in odd ugly chunks like a nattering of angry birds in my head. Stringing them into a meaningful tale is altogether tricky.

My point here is that my lungs never did mend, and I've suffered with the bouts of coughing and the bloody catarrh ever since. 'Tis as clear as horseflies on shite that 'tis always been consumption that I'm suffering these eleven years. 'Tis all in my records, yet the army won't admit any duty toward me for having inflicted it upon me even though 'tis weakened me to the point of rendering me unfit to work.

As for my scattered wits, my black melancholy, and my galumphing Irritable Heart, they simply don't hold that of any account whatsoever.

And now with the new wee girl Julia bore, that makes us a family of ten to house and feed. Four children are my own, and then there are the four from Julia's first husband, though Franky and Mary, thanks be to God, are working down the gingham mill and more than earning their keep. But them toiling away like that only makes my inability to provide all the more shameful for me to bear.

Many's the time I wish I'd never taken a wife. Crippled as I am, I'm a sorry specimen of a man and no good to anyone. I was thirty-three years old when I wed Julia who was a year older than myself. At the time, I was so very lonesome and in need of affection that she did lift my melancholy for a spell. To be direct, I was in dire need of physical comfort and tenderness to take my mind off of my debilitations.

You see, despite the frailty of my lungs, my manhood wasn't hampered in the least and my baser needs were becoming bothersome after a lifetime of abstaining. When I was young, I was rather solitary and shy, so I never courted any lass. That lack of opportunity along with the priests' sermonizing on the mortal sin of fornication and how it could send a soul directly to hell kept me on the straight and narrow path of chastity. When I enlisted at twenty-six, I was still as pure as the driven snow and wasn't at all acquainted with women.

Circumstances changed in a hurry. The camp followers -- Hooker's girls -- were always plentiful in our encampments. Soiled doves in an array of sizes, shapes, colors, and ages, they were nearly always in a state of partial undress, the more to tempt us. I got myself an eyeful many a time, and since they were forthcoming to us shy lads, I had ample opportunity to engage with them. But before I let myself succumb to their vigorous biddings, I perceived how the fellas who had partaken of those ladies' wares were sorely affected afterwards. At the latrine they were well-nigh screaming as they pissed acid and oozed pus. The only relief those poor devils could get was to fortify themselves with whiskey and then visit the surgeon's tent where Doc Gunkle would thrust a horse-sized syringe straight up inside their manly member to dose them with calomel. With dubious results.

Simply ruminating on that grim prospect made me keep my own wick clean and dry and out of trouble. Whenever my privy member was unduly stirred by the vision of those bawdy women and their tempting wares, well, I'd just go off somewhere private and pleasure myself. I knew the priests would claim that a damnable sin, too. But seeing as themselves are doomed to a lifetime of self-denial, I suspected they'd all had occasion to be guilty of the same sin, so I'd be sitting right alongside them in Purgatory.

Anyway, by the time I met Julia in '67, I was beyond lonely for a woman. I was thirty-two and living with my best friend Michael Killian in Gloucester City, New Jersey. After my discharge, I'd been loath to burden William and his family with my keeping in Manayunk, so I'd crossed the Delaware River and boarded with Michael to share our upkeep. Being a mill town, Gloucester City offered many a laboring job, so I was always able to find some kind of work depending on the state of my lungs.

As it happened, my lungs were after giving me a bit of a respite when I met Julia. I'd see her come to Mass with her four wee children, and she always looked so mournful like she had the weight of the world on her slight shoulders. She was short and compact, and though I was usually attracted to taller more robust women, she had fetching curves and a certain switch to her walk that I found enchanting.

So one Sunday morning, I got to the church early and I sat just behind her habitual pew. After Mass was over and we stepped outside, I made sure to be directly behind her. She was struggling a bit with the wee one, Jimmy, who was only four at the time. And didn't that little *spalpeen* take off scarpering directly toward the road. Julia screamed in a panic for him to come back, and before I gave my lungs a second thought, I took off after him.

I caught up to him right as he was headed into the path of a carriage, and as I picked him up he giggled like 'twas all great fun whilst I gulped air a time or two to quiet my over-taxed lungs. I returned him to his mammy, and whilst I watched her scold the *spalpeen*, the look on her face nearly melted my heart. Her big green eyes were both fuming with anger and soft with caring. And when she thanked me, she smiled, and I saw that her teeth were white and straight, like perfect pearls all in a row. Smitten I was.

Well, every Sunday after that, I'd greet her and doff my cap and chuck little Jimmy under the chin, and before long we got to chatting a bit. Eventually, I got up the courage to ask her if I could court her and she agreed.

There was something about Julia that unsettled me in a good way – an underlying ardor she had. Intuition told me she was lonely for a man. And I was beyond lonely for a woman's touch.

One day, after fortifying myself with a couple of whiskeys, I asked her to marry me, promising her that I'd provide for her children as if they were my very own. To my astonishment she agreed, and we wed on the first day of March in '68.

Mortified I am to admit it, but I was the timorous one on our wedding night. Here she'd been married for ten years to her first husband and birthed five children, and I'd never bedded a woman. I was fearful I wouldn't be up to the task.

But Julia made it real easy. She was eager, which dispelled my trepidation. Nature just took over and there was no problem at all. In fact, 'twas that very first night that I planted Sarah's seed, for she came just scant of nine months later. I wondered how I'd gone so long without what only comes natural between two people harboring a mutual affection and the need to escape from life's toilsome misery for a time.

So 'twas happy we were those first few years, while my lungs still had some life to them and I was able to work fairly steady. We were only too delighted when Sarah was born, and then Eamon. But by the time Denny was born, Julia and I were feeling the strain of the children's upkeep, for I was working less and less while Julia was getting none the younger. And now

Maggie is here. But being that we're both the worse for wear, we can't take much joy in her wee self.

JULIA

I was always after thinking that men are a fairly simple lot. Give a fella work for his hands, food for his belly, and a woman to warm his bed, and he's as happy as a lark singing in the meadow. Leastways that's how my darling James was.

But my Samuel is a different creature altogether. He's baffling and gloomy, downright daft at times. His mood changes from joy to sorrow as quickly as a draft will blow out a candle. And he's given to such black brooding about things folks have no business pondering at all, puzzling things that are best left to the higher ups to sort out, such a ones as the priests who the Church in her great wisdom has allotted to teach us simpler souls.

And he's forever throwing them highfalutin words around – words he gets from his books – like he's a poet of standing or the lord of the manor. And though I've picked up a few of them lofty words myself and found them right handy, I only use them when they fit my meaning and don't never toss them around like as if I'm putting on the airs.

When we was first wedded, he tried to foist the book learning on me, singing the praises of reading and how 'tis a needed skill. And though I was shamed that I couldn't read nor write, I had a house and children to care for and another baby on the way, so's I couldn't waste no time untangling all them black squiggles and then piecing them back together again to make words. 'Twas beyond my ken as I was getting too long in the tooth to be able to keep all them letters straight in my head.

Even so, I'm gratified that my children have learnt to read in school where their young minds picked it up quick. I see the book learning rubbing off on Mary and Jimmy, my serious, clever children that I had with my darling James. Mary is fifteen and Jimmy, my brightest one, is nine and they are always after craving the books, which of course are too dear for us to even think of buying. Samuel lets them read his Pa's books, but only when he's right there to oversee their handling as Samuel cherishes them books more than anything in the world. Even more than me and the babies it seems like.

Then didn't he go and tell them two that across the river in Philadelphia there is a lending library full of thousands of books to borrow, that he used to go there anytime he liked and come away with armfuls that he'd read every night afore sleep. I think 'twas a cruel thing to do since here in Gloucester City there is nary a one lending library. Which is all for the good since them two would be at the books every hour of the day when they need to be keeping themselves busy with more useful tasks about the house.

I can't complain about my Mary; she's good as gold with the wee ones. Nothing would please her more than to be staying to home, helping me tend them all the livelong day and then spending the evening with her nose buried in a book. But since Samuel can't hardly get no work, I had to send her to join her brother Franky toiling in the gingham mill all the livelong days to help in keeping ourselves fed. The poor girl's after being ragged when she gets back home, not fit for naught but a quick meal and sleep. And the lint that clouds the mill's workrooms troubles Mary's lungs which worries me no end.

Thanks be to God, the lint don't bother my Franky who's hale and hardworking like his Pa, James. He's sixteen and don't mind the work at all. Jesus Mary and Joseph, if 'tweren't for them two earning the wages, we'd surely all be out on the street. Since the money panic last year, folks have been frugal so my seamstress duties have fell off, but I still earn the odd bit here and there for which I'm grateful.

Now my Kate who is twelve is a worry. If I wasn't the good Catholic woman I am and was after believing in pagan tales, I'd swear that girl was a changeling swapped out for my real baby by the *aos si* -- for she does naught but giggle and frolic all the livelong day. She had trouble learning in school, so's her reading and ciphering is poor. When she turned ten, I finally kept her to home as the schooling wasn't doing her no good since she can't keep nary a thought in that silly head of hers but it leaks straight out. She's never after being serious nor paying attention to what she's about, always behind like the tail of the cow, so's I fret to think what is to become of her.

Along with those aforementioned living children from James, there are the added four babies myself and Samuel had together which are still such a young brood what needs a ma's endless care. Our eldest, Sarah, is not yet six years old and is Samuel all over again, more's the pity. She's got his sorrowful face and his striking blue eyes which are lovely indeed, but she's also fraught with his melancholy ways and already after fretting and brooding over everything. Them two is bonded tight for they understand one another's queerness.

Our Eamon just turned four, and he takes after me - spindly but hale and already has my steady ways. Little Denny is but two, so the darling *spalpeen* is headstrong as that age always is and he's always needing the looking after. Jesus Mary and Joseph, but I'm needing the eyes on the back of my head to keep up with that one's antics.

Wee Maggie just three months old is by far my prettiest baby with her mop of curly dark hair and big sea-green eyes that remind me so of my brother Daniel's. But she's not fattening up like she should. It may be my milk is turned old and sour, for she's never took to the breast like the others, just sucks a time or two and turns her head away to wail and pull up the legs in pain. Fretful and colicky with the runny flux now and then, she's suckling in dribs and drabs, which is a great worry to me. I'm walking her up and down the floor all the livelong day and night trying to keep the poor thing settled and keep her from her pitiful wailing.

Beyond weary I am. I told Samuel there won't be no more babies for me. I was never a one to stint my wifely duties – with neither of my two husbands. 'Tis a good Catholic woman's duty to submit to her husband's needs. Afore Maggie, I never minded the coupling; I even relished it now and again. But more's the pity, I'm as fruitful as my own ma, so every time my James or Samuel unbuttoned their trousers, they'd get me with child.

When Maggie was born, the midwife told me my womb is wore out, sagging and not able to hold any more babies safely to birth. And I know she's right since I can feel the dropping of it. 'Tis no surprise after bearing nine, and myself being nigh on forty as far as I can reckon. Samuel wasn't much upset. What with his health going to bits, I don't think he much cares about such things no more.

I've got my hands full what with babies to tend to and ten hungry mouths to feed and a husband not fit to work more than the odd time. Samuel has always suffered a bit of feebleness and constraint from the bullet wounds, but lately 'tis the consumption that's lying him low again. He gets into these piteous states with the gasping and the coughing up of the blood. 'Tis a sorrowful sight altogether and there's naught to be done about it but to feed him the marrow broth and the eggs 'til he can get his strength back to be after doing some work once again.

Sure and he's a sickly man. But what I can't pardon him for is his queer melancholy state of mind that leads to the black brooding. 'Tis always made him a bit of a malingerer, even when his lungs was fit for the work. 'Tis his faintness of will that don't let Samuel escape that devilish war that ended ten years ago. Many's the soldier who has banished all that ugliness and gone on with his day-to-day living, but Samuel sinks to reviving the war's worst visions day in and day out.

God forgive me, I know he's more to be pitied than scorned what with his nightmares and terror-filled eyes, but how can I pity a one who's got the vigor to get me with four babies in six years but not keep to steady work?

Now as I've said afore, my first husband James was a sturdy fella, strong and fit from wielding them blacksmith's tools all the livelong day. 'Tis only natural he'd be robust at the begetting. But all the while I've been wedded to Samuel, his mind and body have been crumbling to bits excepting for that manly part of his body that makes the babies which always works just fine. I pray to Our Blessed Lady that now that I'm not letting him put his manly part to no more use with me, some of that vigor will go to his lungs.

If I'm after being truthful, I've only myself to blame. Samuel was suffering the consumption when I met him, and I've pondered was I soft in the head to go and wed him. But I couldn't live on my brother's charity forever. The dressmaking wasn't bringing in enough money for to support my babies, and that meant I needed a husband. Trouble was, there wasn't scarcely no whole-bodied, unwedded men left alive after the war. 'Twas just the old men and boys. I wasn't about to wed no old gnarly thing nor rob the cradle, so pickings was slim indeed.

When I met Samuel two years after my James died, it seemed a true Godsend. 'Specially since 'twas a miracle the way Samuel saved my wee Jimmy from certain calamity when he run out into the road directly in front of a carriage and Samuel scooped him up out of harm's way. 'Twasn't like Jimmy, my clever one, to be such a naughty *spalpeen*, so it seemed like a sign from God Himself. And though that might be neither here nor there, I surely owed Samuel a great deal.

So 'twas after he saved my Jimmy so valiantly that I peered closely into Samuel's face. What with that honey-gold hair of his and them cornflower blue eyes that shone out his face like as if they were lighted from inside, I thought to myself now he's not bad looking at all. More important, he's after being a decent, clean, Catholic man. And just as I was pondering these thoughts, didn't he give me his shy smile - not so rare to his face then as 'tis now. 'Twas like a balm to my grieving widow's heart.

To tell the truth, I was flattered that he paid me any mind what with all of the fresh young maidens clambering for any man they could find amongst the war leavings. Samuel was willing to settle for me though I was already a bit long in the tooth being about thirty-three and burdened with the four wee ones. But in spite of all of my birthing, I'd a trim figure on me and all of my teeth still in my head, which I reckon balanced things off a bit.

Now back then, Samuel wasn't suffering all that much, just had the coughing fits and the spitting up bits of blood now and again, which counted for next to naught what with all them other fellas hobbling about missing the legs and the arms and even bits of their faces. 'Twas a right pity to see. And some was clearly out their wits with their peculiar ramblings and loud carryings-on. And as I said afore, I was more than grateful to him for saving my Jimmy's life.

More's the pity, I had nary an inkling about the melancholy broods Samuel would sink into from time to time, the mournful bitterness that overtook him at them times. 'Twasn't 'til after we was married a few months that I observed his dark side. Now in this last year what with his lungs troubling him so bad, these black times of his have come upon him all the more, sinking him into ever deeper melancholy. It scares me something fierce, making me to wonder did I do the right thing when I wed him, or did I just add the extra burden onto my shoulders.

If I knew then what I know now, would I do it again? Though I do love the four babies he's given me, am I after needing all that care and worry they bring? And am I as fond of Samuel as a wife should be? I never did love him like I loved my darling James who was after being too good to be true. God forgive me, the regret overcomes me at times.

I will put this foolishness from my mind. What is past is past and can't be undone. God blessed me with haleness and fortitude, and with His help I will tend to the present without no more brooding.

SAMUEL

The thing is, Julia and I are not of the same mind. I'd not known her long enough before I wed her to discern her true nature. What I took to be strength was downright mulishness. And whilst I turn a deaf ear to half of what the priests say as so much blather, Julia is overly pious and believes every bit of drivel that comes out their gobs as if handed down from God himself. Worst of all, she can be such a scald.

Many's the time I rue the day we wed. A bachelor I should've remained without obligation to a wife and children whose very presence rebuke me with my shortcomings. I reckon that in my awful loneliness, I was simply beguiled by Julia's comeliness, her womanliness. 'Twas my manly needs that got the better of me.

'Tis altogether sad, but Julia is not one for the books as she can't read nor write and has no interest in learning. Early on, I tried to teach her, and beyond patient I was. But she wanted no part of it. Can you imagine? Not wanting to read? Not wanting to imbibe all those enchanting words? Not wanting to acquire knowledge? And her mangling of grammar sets my very teeth on edge; 'tis like the fingernail scraping on the slate.

She is not a stupid woman, yet she prefers to live in a shroud of ignorance so she doesn't have to ponder the distasteful bits of life. 'Tis easier for her to trust the priests implicitly and attribute any event be it joyful or sad to an act of God that cannot be changed by any living being no matter how well educated he may be. I cannot fathom such backwardness of mind.

Worse still, she begrudges me my time spent reading as she chides me that I should be out after earning a living, herself having little sympathy for my ailments. Now, 'tis clear as horseflies on shite that I am an ailing man. What with my unrelenting wheezing and coughing and feverishness and general feebleness I won't make old bones. Yet she's always on about how I need to find work to feed the babies.

And as for babies, had I known Julia was still after being as fertile as a hare though she was older than me when we wed, I'd have run the other way. Four babes in six years, you'd think I was on her every night instead of the twice or thrice a week as any normal fella does. And now since Maggie came, she's begrudging me even the odd bit of coupling I'm after needing as 'tis the only remedy to confound her fruitfulness.

As for her scolding, 'twas just this morning that I looked up from my reading the newspaper and wasn't she after fixing me with her blackest look.

"Jesus Mary and Joseph," she chided me, "youse got the nose in the paper again! The four cents youse wasted on that could've bought the bottle of milk."

"Quit with the nattering! I didn't have to pay for it. 'Twas Benny down the tavern who was after giving it to me."

"And what were youse doing down the tavern this time of day?"

"'Twasn't drinking I was doing! I was after asking about a bit of easy work. And why would you begrudge me the bit of reading when 'tis the only solace left to me?"

"Yeah, youse and your precious books! Youse may be feeding off them pages, but them little black marks aren't after filling our babies' bellies."

"What are you on about? We're not starving!"

"We would be if 'twasn't for my Mary and Franky toiling down the mill. We'd be starving and out on the street."

"For the love of God, woman! Do you not see the state of me? I can't be after crossing the room without coughing up bits of my lung. How am I to find work with one foot in the very grave?"

"Arrah, what are youse on about? You're fit enough to want to be filling me with more babies!"

"Evil woman, you're the heartscald to me! 'You know 'tis been only the odd time I've been hale enough to bother you at the begetting business." I gave her the black look. "And now you've turned me away forever. Not that I mind, since I'd not be touching the likes of you, you cold, begrudging shrew!"

She peered at me then, and I saw wounded pride and perhaps a flicker of remorse in her cool green eyes. She turned and headed to the hob where the kettle was steaming.

"Are youse after wanting your tea now?" she said by way of contrition.

Then wasn't it my wee Sarah who piped in, "I'll get it for him, Ma."

There she stood, my little *mavourneen*, looking on the both of us with her worried blue eyes as big as platters. She's but six years old and already after carrying the weight of the world on her thin shoulders. Quiet as a mouse, she always appears during my squabbles with Julia trying her utmost to set us at peace. Her being my first born, she's always been my favorite. And more's the pity, she takes after me in looks and melancholy temperament though she's got her mammy's wee size.

Seeing the poor little dear trying to set us aright brought Julia and myself both to shame that knocked the rancor right out of us.

"'Tis alright, Darlin," said Julia, patting Sarah on the noggin. "Youse go keep an eye on our Denny whilst I fetch your Pa his tea."

Julia turned away, and I motioned for Sarah to come to me. I put my arm around her thin self and peered into her woeful eyes.

"Ah *mavourneen*. Your mammy and I shouldn't have been at the quarreling. We didn't mean to be unkind to one another. 'Tis my ailments that make us cross."

"You said you're near to the grave, Pa. Are you going to die?" she whispered, the tears glistering in her eyes.

"Ah child, I'm sick to be sure, but I'm not ready to be going just yet."

I pulled her close, and she nuzzled into my chest. She sobbed a bit as I kissed the top of her glossy-haired head which smelled of soap and woodfire. After several moments, I let go and told her, "Off you go now, and keep a keen eye on wee Denny like your mammy told you. He's forever getting into the mischief."

"Yes Pa," she snuffled and wiped her runny nose with the back of her hand.

Just then Julia came back with the tea, and Sarah looked on the both of us.

"Please don't be after the squabbling," she whimpered. "It hurts my heart."

She turned and went to tend to her brother. Julia and I sat with our heads bowed over our teacups, unable to look on one another for the shame of it.

PART TWO

1876 - 1879

JULIA

'Tis been two years now since I birthed my Maggie. She's finally gone off the breast and I'm only too delighted to have my body all to myself these days. After nigh on twenty years, I was beyond weary of the business of one babe dancing a jig in my belly whilst another one was setting on my hip or lapping away at my breasts.

Thanks be to Our Blessed Virgin those days are behind me. At my age, I'm more than content to do without none of the pawing and poking of a lusty husband. I count my blessings that out of nine children I've buried just the one, my firstborn my little Johnny, who's lying directly aside his Pa in the graveyard. May the earth lie gently on them. My two best ones.

But 'tis hard to be easy in my mind what with my Samuel faring so poorly. He's just past forty, but shrinking and shriveling so he looks to be ancient. He's sinking in body and mind -- coughing up the bloody gouts, wheezing and gasping for air, running the fevers. The state of him is pitiful, and he's not getting hardly no lulls like he used to when he got well enough to be after earning the odd bit of pay.

Adding to our troubles, there's his slipping more and more into the black broods that last for days when there's no talking to him, he'll not reply. He sets in the chair aside the fire, gawps at naught or nods off to a fitful slumber only to wake up with a screech and the look of a haunt or a madman in his eyes.

Last year, more's the pity, we moved across the river here to Philadelphia where we have the three wee rooms upstairs in a boarding house just down from the river on Race Street. I was sore to leave Gloucester City for this noisome place, but Samuel was after having a lull in the consumption and had the notion that there'd be the opportunity of good paying work down the docks of such a busy city where they're always after looking for help. I thought he was daft, for there was jobs aplenty in Gloucester City, but so pleased was I that he was finally looking to stir his stumps and earn steady money, I swallowed my doubts.

But no sooner did we move here then the state of himself took a big turn for the worse. He's not been fit to work no more than the odd time here or there when he's recovered his wits and breath some. And now it seems even them days are gone forever.

He's still after trying to get a fair pension from the army since 'twas that war that made such short shrift of his body and his mind. Bullets rendered one arm feeble and his other hand's pointer finger all crookedy and scarred with webbing, so's he can't be after bending it. So even if his lungs ease up so he can breathe, he's still got the troubles lifting the crates or barrels or gripping the shovel or pick axe.

But the crux of the matter is the army won't pay no mind to the state of his lungs even though 'twas while soldiering that he come down with the consumption. Himself having to slog and sleep through all weathers, 'tis no wonder. But the army still won't give Samuel no more than a pittance -- two dollars a month for a family of nine! Even after he got himself a fancy lawyer over by the riverside on Front Street to fight for him. Many's the time Samuel, on his last legs, traipsed the dozen blocks down to Mr. Poulson's office for that rapscallion promised to get him his due, but all for naught.

Now there's some folks who do well for themselves in America. My brother Daniel for one, and Samuel's brother William for another. They've both got the steady work and the grand pay. But neither of them two had their strength bled away fighting in that daft war so's they're both after being hale and hearty. And whilst them two get to use their noggins more than their brawn to earn their pay, their heads are clear and sound. My poor Samuel hasn't neither the vigorous body nor the sound mind all on account of fighting for a cause that had naught to do with the likes of us.

As 'tis, we're getting by with the half-filled bellies and the tattered clothes. The children are all after needing shoes and mine are a-flapping wide open at the toes.

More's the pity, we should've stayed in Gloucester City where our lodgings was cheaper and I had the odd bit of seamstress earnings and Mary earned a useful bit down the mill. Here in Philadelphia, I hardly bring in no money myself as my seamstress days are all but done. I don't hardly know no one, and 'tis such a big city there's a dressmaker's shop on every block. So's I only get the odd mending job now and again and the two loads of laundry I take in a week as that's all I can handle in my washtub.

We sorely miss Mary's earnings, though her lungs are the better for leaving the mill. She's sixteen now and I could send her out to service with a rich household, but 'twould be a Protestant family no doubt. Father O'Donnell is always after warning us about the danger of

Protestant householders depriving their Catholic servants of Sunday mornings free to attend Mass, thereby turning them heretic. I'd not put my Mary's soul in such grievous jeopardy. And how could I part with her? I'd sorely miss her and all the help she is with the chores and tending the wee ones.

So 'tis that we're after barely getting by on Samuel's pension, my laundry pennies, and the odd bit my Franky can spare to send us. He didn't come across the river with us since he found himself a sweetheart and a grand job as a teamster for a shipyard back in Gloucester City. He's eighteen now and strong as an ox like his Pa, and such a Dearie to be helping us out whilst paying his own way and saving the pennies to get married.

But whilst I'm on the tenterhooks worrying my head over how to buy the food after paying the rent, Samuel sets in his chair wrapped up to his chin in the quilts, woolgathering or dozing. I can abide that, since he's clearly ailing. But when he gets into one of them black broods, or worse yet, to reading his Daddy's books and goes off into a daze with nary a thought to our needs, I break out in a fury. How can he lose himself inside them books like that and not worry none about the dire straits we've fallen into?

We two is always after squabbling about it and got ourselves into a right ugly quarrel this morning. I told him, "Youse need to put that book down and apply your mind to finding a new lawyer, a right smart one who'll do his job, not like that lazy Poulson one, bad *cess* to him."

"Lay off with your nattering Julia, we've been through all this before!" said he. "Poulson is the man to see if you're after needing the pension. 'Tis not his fault, 'tis the government not taking responsibility for my lungs no matter how bad they get. There's naught he nor any other lawyer can do."

"So's you'll just set there reading, getting lost in the fairy tales whilst your children are wanting for the food and the clothes."

"For the love of God, do you not see the state of me? I'm nearing death's very door. Grant me some peace in my last days!"

And then he broke into the gagging and coughing and gasping. He couldn't hardly get no breath, and his lips was turning blue. 'Twas the worst I'd ever seen him. Affrighted I was, for he was the picture of my James and Johnny as they smothered to death before my very eyes.

Alarmed, I went to comfort him, rubbing his boney back and cooing to him like he was one of my sick babies. He was gurgling, so I gave him his tin cup that he keeps by his side and he spit a great gout of blood into it, then wiped his mouth with his hanky, smearing the bloody drool along his chin. He was feverish and shaking like as if his very bones was ice, his face a picture of suffering.

"Give me them," I gentled my voice as I reached for the cup and the hanky and swabbed his chin clean. Helpless as a babe he was, for he hadn't no vigor for to push me away as a grown man ought to do.

I turned my face as the tears welled in my eyes, for I'd not let him see me crying as 'twould hurt his pride something fierce to know he's become such a piteous sight. I washed his cup and fetched him a clean hanky and draped the quilt around his frail and bowed shoulders. I remember them being wide and strong not seven years past.

Himself looked at me with such sorrowful eyes, it brought me to shame for my naggling at him.

"Arrah Samuel, beyond sorry I am for nattering at youse. 'Twas shameful of me. I know youse is only doing your best. 'Tis just that I'm at wits end with the worrying."

I kissed his brow and the heat coming off it set my heart to racing.

"Youse is after needing a drop of opium in the blackest tea to settle them lungs. 'Tis steeping now and will be good and strong enough to walk a mouse across it in just a wee minute."

I fetched the tea, stirred in a extra drop of the opium, and made him drink every bit, then put him to bed.

Mother of God, what a state we're in. Samuel suffering such agony and not long for this world, and us living on a pittance. There's naught to be done but to be at the prayers morning noon and night asking for deliverance.

SAMUEL

Jesus Mary and Joseph. What's a man to do? 'Tis ashamed I am to be nothing but a burden to Julia and the children when I'm the one 'tis supposed to be providing for them. Now 'tis Franky who's sending us the odd pennies, and it shames me something fierce to be taking the charity from my stepson. I'm so feeble and my wits are after going astray for days at a time so I can't be figuring my way out of this predicament.

I'm so broken inside; I can't find myself among all the scattered bits. Bewildered I am and disordered. I sit here, rise up out of myself and I watch my family all about me as if I'm watching strangers on a stage. Wee Eamon, Denny and Maggie are at their play whilst Jimmy and Sarah are at their schoolwork, Kate is woolgathering as is her wont, and Mary is helping Julia with the chores, but they're miles away from me and pay me no mind. I don't know them at all, not even Julia. I can't reach a one of them. 'Tis like I'm trapped behind a window, peering through the glass at my family as they're carrying on without a glance my way. 'Tis like I'm dead but worse, for being dead would be peaceful oblivion.

'Tis morbid Julia says I am, for I ponder death more than any sound man should. But I consider it a blessing. Many a dead man I've seen in the aftermath of a savage battle, and though he may have had the stiff grimace or the frozen howling mouth, 'twas clear that his genuine self had long since departed and was past suffering by the time I beheld his bloated, flyblown corpse. Aside from Ezra whose dear face was blasted clear off, of the countless men I've seen in the very act of dying -- even those who suffered the worst agony -- at the very last moment their faces smoothed over in peace as though a soothing mammy's hand had brushed the pain away. I'd like to think 'tis the door to Heaven they spy for I'd like to trust it exists.

Yet, if there is no Heaven where we can be with our lost loved ones, then 'tis surely just the blissful, dreamless sleep which we've earned that awaits us.

As for Hell, 'tis nonsense. Nothing can be worse than our suffering here on earth, and no priest will sway me otherwise. They would have us believe that Hell's eternal torments lie in store for many the decent sort who slip up the odd time. For if you miss the one Sunday Mass, or in a fit of agony call out God's name in vain, or eat a sausage on the Friday, you'll burn forevermore. As if God would bother Himself with such fripperies!

And then the priests further terrify us with their tales of Purgatory. For even if we do confess these sins and the priests magically cleanse them away so we're saved from hellfire, we're still after going headlong to a hot time in Purgatory to render our souls pure as the driven snow.

No. I'll not believe in Hell nor Purgatory. Our life on earth is filled with endless suffering and woe; I'll not be duped by those high-in-the-head priests who pontificate their dire warnings to keep us under their thumbs.

Hence, 'tis not the dying I fear. 'Tis living that is my daily sufferance, for in addition to my agonies of body and mind I'm naught but a burden and a hindrance to my family. This morning I roused myself to perform some sorely needed ablutions which I had been neglecting due to my poor state, and as I readied myself to shave -- stropping the razor beyond sharp -- I pondered once again how easy 'twould be to make short shrift of my useless self. One quick swipe from ear to ear would do it in a trice.

Many's the time I've contemplated this. Yet I can't perform the gory deed at home. 'Twould be cruel beyond measure for my children to find my body with its lolling head dribbling blood into a great pool. Yet I haven't the fortitude to take myself down the road to a back alley alongside the river for the odd stranger to find me.

The opium (which Doc Saunders in his kindness gives me without charge on account of my service to the Union) mixed in my tea calms the chest, but not the mind. 'Tis queer how it works. Though it makes me drowsy, it also sets me on edge, agitates me, makes my waking nightmares more vivid and fearful.

'Tis befuddled I am. Aside from doing away with myself, there's naught I can do but endure whilst hoping I recuperate enough to work and be of some use, to pull my strayed wits together and be a man once again. Else die in the bed in my sleep.

JULIA

Thanks be to God Samuel is having a bit of a respite from the consumption. These last few days his fever is gone and his cough is easing and he's been eating the eggs and the broth, been up and about which always manages to steady his wits some. 'Tis odd this coming and going of his sickness, him being at death's very door for a month or two and then his rallying enough to have a clearer mind and do the odd job so's he can be after bringing home the few pennies. 'Tis been like that the entire time I've known him. But 'tis clearly getting worse, for each time his fevered bouts last longer and his recoveries are shorter and render him less hale.

I know he's only trying his best, though I can't help but fret about the coming of his next bout, for his respites never last long. Off to work he is for the odd day or two and then he's back lying flat in the bed or hunched in the chair aside the fire, dog-tired and with the feverish red spots on his cheeks. He's bonier, less sinewy, slowly wasting away is what he's after doing. There's naught he nor nobody else can do. Doc Saunders says 'tis the way of the consumption, Samuel could last five more years or he could go tomorrow. All I can do is get the eggs and the marrow broth into him, dose him with the opium, and keep him warm.

I know I need to leave off with the nattering. It disturbs the children and sets us all on edge. I catch Sarah, who's never a one to be saucy, giving me the black look each time I get to griping at him, her blue eyes turning cold and hard as glass. She's just after turning nine years old, but you'd think she was an old granny the way she frets, especially over her Pa. She's always looking to his comfort and always takes his side, for she's always been his favorite, her being his spit and all.

And then didn't Eamon whisper to me just the other day, "Ma, why are youse always after yelling at the Pa when he's so sick?" Shamed me he did, and him being but seven years old.

"Arrah Dearie, 'tis not your Pa I'm angry at," I told him. "'Tis his bad lungs that get me vexed and worried, and then the worst of me shows itself."

"Can't Doc Saunders mend him?"

"There's naught to be done Dearie, his lungs is all wore out past mending."

"How'd they get so wore out?"

"Was soldiering that done it, marching and lying in the wet and the cold."

"Why'd Pa do that? Go soldiering?"

"He needed the steady pay and thought he was after doing his country a service."

"I'll not go for the soldiering when I grow up." Eamon's wee face was filled with the resolve.

"That's a great relief to your Ma," I told him and patted his head. "And for that I'll leave off the nattering at your Pa."

He hugged me. And as he went his way, I resolved to put a lid on my too-quick temper and wayward tongue.

But 'tis not just Samuel I fret over that brings on my temper. There's my two youngest that was born with the weight of the clay on them, not hale like my others. Maybe I was too old when I bore them, my body too wore out to give them what they needed when they was growing inside me.

Little Denny's always got the dripping nose and the smudges 'neath the eyes like as if someone pressed sooty thumbs there. I mostly worry after his lungs for he's always after having the rales with the coughing. Doc Saunders says 'tis just the catarrh and he'll grow out of it, but

I'm not after being soothed. 'Specially since he's got the prickly appetite and I can't hardly get nothing down him so he's spindly as a bundle of sticks.

And Maggie my prettiest babe who takes after my people with her sea-green eyes and glossy red-brown curls is such a touchy thing, naught at all like my others. The least noise startles her and sets her to crying. I can't look on her crossways or she'll take to sobbing. Every wee bruise and scratch sets her to wailing like 'tis a death wound. She's but three, so's I hope she'll soon be after bolstering up for if not she'll never make it through this life of care. I pray she finds herself a gentle husband to coddle her and keep her safe.

Many's the time I can't fathom my family's wants -- though one brood they're all as different as can be. But I try hard to stretch the pennies to get the best victuals for them, the richest marrow-filled beef bones for to make the broth, and the freshest eggs. But the better the food, the dearer the cost. And though we're barely getting by, we'll not be begging off our brothers. Daniel and William are making the grand pay and would never begrudge us, but they've their own families to see to, and Samuel and I haven't sunk so low as to hold out open hands and act the tinkers.

No, we'll manage. I'll keep up by finding the odd seamstress job. Meantime, I go down the road on the Mondays gathering the dirty linens from Mrs. Rutherford and Mrs. Oglesby for to bring back and launder in our washtub and hang on the line out our window in the alleyway. 'Tis honest work and I'm not too proud though 'tis heavy toil for not much more than a pittance, but better than be after the begging.

I often think back to my days with my darling James when I had naught a worry, for we had the cozy house and the warm clothes and plenty of fresh food on the table. 'Twas the only time in my life I wasn't after scrabbling for them things.

And my James was clear-headed and hale, so's we two enjoyed the chatting and the laughing and even the teasing now and again, for 'twas all in fun. We was of one mind in so many matters, like two peas in a pod. Ten years of joy and prosperity out of my forty-odd years of living. Now 'tis nigh on another ten years with Samuel. Yet I don't think I've ever known the man.

Though 'tis no good to liken my husbands for there's naught good can come of it, I can't help recalling that even though my James could read and write, 'twas only the odd newspaper he cared about. I can't recall him ever reading a book, and he surely never owned a one. Yet Samuel gets lost in them to forego his duty, which I am hard-pressed to forgive.

Jesus Mary and Joseph, them books of his! The more he's after ailing, the more he sinks his face into them. How many times can a one read a book? There's just the three fat ones he's after having from his Daddy and worn they are since he can't leave them be. 'Tis shameful how he treasures them like nothing else, even more than me and his very own children. After all these years he must have the words by heart, so what's the use of him keeping them books anyway?

SAMUEL

Beyond the beyond I am with rage. I reckon if 'tweren't for my feebleness I'd be after throttling her stringy neck. That viper of a woman who vowed to be true to me in sickness and in health has betrayed me in the vilest way.

It sickens me so I can barely be about the telling of it. Last evening, I was particularly melancholy, my spirits being way down in the deepest pit of despair. During those bleakest of times, I find that Donne's Meditations can bring me a small measure of calming comfort. But when I went to fetch my Daddy's Donne from the cupboard, I found it and my other books had all vanished!

"Julia!" I wailed, "where have you put my books?" I was hoping against hope that she'd moved them whilst at the cleaning, though she knew better than to disturb them. And when I saw the shameful look on her face, I feared the worst.

"Arrah," she said, all twitchy and not daring to look me in the eye. "The children is after needing the woolens and the shoes to face the winter months, so didn't I take them books down Mr. Middleton's. And didn't that grand man give me three whole dollars for the lot, shabby as them things were!"

There she stood, wringing her guilty hands and giving out the shamefaced little laugh.

As I looked on her revolting self, the rage engulfed me so entirely that 'twas several seconds before I could reply. Then I gave it full vent, not caring what perturbation I caused.

"You wicked, evil woman! You stupid, ignorant slattern!" I fairly bellowed, giving not a thought to children nor neighbor overhearing.

I positively convulsed with rage and 'twas all I could do not to smash my fist into her face, for I found it intolerable to behold. She froze with a look of pure fear, for I'd never spoken to her in such a harsh way before. And I must have been quite the terrible sight. But her fright of me did nothing to ease my fury.

"Damn you, you thieving thing! Damn you! Skulking behind my back to rob me of my inheritance! Pilfering my own dear Daddy's books only to peddle them away for mere coinage! The very ones he cherished so deeply he wouldn't trade them away during the worst of The Hunger!"

Trembling, she stood stock still and gawped on me, for I'd never cursed her nor any living soul within her hearing before.

Mightily I struggled to becalm my anger so as to calculate the situation, to focus my mind on finding a solution. There was but one. I glared on her revolting face, lowering my voice to a cold dictate.

"You will undo your foul deed. First thing tomorrow morning, you will take your Judas money back to Mr. Middleton and get Daddy's books back even if you have to get down on your knees and beg."

She gawped on me as though she couldn't understand a word I said which made me altogether more furious.

"Did you hear me, you viper?" I bellowed. "First thing in the morning!"

"I can't," she whined, and took a step back as if she expected me to strike her. "I spent the money already, down Sander's general store on the children's necessities I told youse about and for a store of victuals for to get us through the next month. 'Twas no betrayal as all is sorely needed!"

"'Twas betrayal indeed, for you never consulted me, but stole them away when my back was turned. Besides, there was no need, for you can get our necessities on credit."

"No, I can't! 'Tis the very point! Mr. Sanders said our credit's no good no more! We already owed him five dollars, so after I begged him for leniency, he agreed to settle on taking the one dollar toward our debt as long as I paid cash for the rest. But he'll only be taking the cash from now on – 'til we pay off the lingering four dollars. That's why I had to sell them books."

This was a blow I hadn't foreseen, but 'twouldn't change my determination to set things to right.

"Then tomorrow morning we'll be after returning all of the things you bought from Mr. Sanders, get the money back, and then we'll be going to Mr. Middleton and getting Daddy's books back."

"Have youse even been listening to me, youse great big lump? Mr. Sanders won't be giving us any money back when we still owe him the four dollars!"

I saw the dreadful truth in her words and struggled to find a workable solution.

"Alright then. As you leave me no choice, I'll be the beggar and write to William to loan me the money. I'll pay him back from your laundry pennies. Tomorrow morning, I will visit Mr.

Middleton and tell him to hold those books until Friday when I will buy them back."

"Youse will do no such thing!" Julia was up on her high horse now. "Your mind is all a-muddle, youse are not after thinking straight at all. I'm the one has to see to the feeding and caring of our brood. I work my back to aching and my fingers raw to bleeding at doing the laundry so's this family can eat! I'll not turn those dearly earned pennies over to pay a debt to your brother just so's youse can have them old wore out books for to be reading whilst your children starve!"

Her obdurate face was as hard as granite, her chin jutted forward, and her eyes icy green. Her lack of remorse spurred my fury.

"What would you be knowing about books, you ignorant *amadan* who refused all my efforts to enlighten your shameful backwardness?"

Her face crumpled at the insult, but she shouted, "I may be unlettered, but I've the decency to know 'tis my duty to provide for my babies, youse lazy *louser*! And I won't be letting youse take no food out my babies' mouths, neither! 'Specially not for the sake of some old moldy bits of paper! Them books may have fed youse, but they didn't keep the hunger from my children's bellies!"

"My children have never suffered from want, and you know it! You're just after begrudging me my only consolation. There's no more to be said. We are getting Daddy's books back by whatever means we must."

"Youse are a wicked, selfish man, Samuel!" Her green eyes blazed fury like I'd never seen. "Youse love them useless books more than youse love your very own children! Curse the day I married such a malingering lout!"

She stalked into our bed chamber and slammed the door behind her. I stood there trembling with disgust and fury, regretting that our marriage had come to such a pretty pass.

I turned and saw my stepson Jimmy giving me a look of pure hatred, his fists tight at his side. Mary and the children were huddled together by the fireside, their eyes wide with fear. Ashamed at what I must have looked to them and knowing not what to say, I turned and wandered down the stairs and sat upon the stoop.

And here I remain, contemplating my abysmal state. I am so very weary with sickness and woe and the battling with Julia. I pray I can get Daddy's books back, for when I fall into the blackest despair, they are the only things that touch me, that grant me a semblance of comfort. Just clasping them, feeling the smooth, worn leather, becalms my restless mind as nothing else can. My Daddy comes back to me, the sight and sound of him reading. In losing them I've lost all touch with my Daddy and my former self.

If I can't have them back, I'll not ever forgive her.

JULIA

I'm affeared I've broken things past all mending, though 'twasn't my intent to do a wrong, but to set a wrong to rights. For my children are after needing the warm clothes and shoes, and I was only after seeing to their wants which is my motherly duty. 'Tis true, I should have asked Samuel afore I sold his books, but I knew he'd not allow it, so what was the point?

Didn't Samuel become the madman when he found out. In a rage he was, like I've never seen him. He even cursed me, something I never thought I'd hear come out his Catholic mouth. And then it pained me something fierce when he called me a ignorant slattern. Worse still when he called me wicked and likened me to Judas! I'm not wicked, and though I am unlettered, I'm not after being foolish nor stupid. He had no call to talk to me like that. 'Twas not wicked deceit, but motherly care that drove me. As for him calling me a thief, 'tis not true, for wedded folk own all things in common.

Worse, he afrighted the children witless. There they was a-cowering by the fire, the little ones huddled together like a litter of quaking pups, whilst my Mary shielded them as if to ward off the devil himself.

Then didn't my Jimmy, he's fourteen now, didn't he come up behind Samuel and bellow, "Leave my Ma alone, you bully!"

But 'twas like wind blowing over top Samuel's head. He never even heard, just kept roaring away. I couldn't hardly believe his lungs was fit for such shouting. Jimmy took a step closer and I feared he would strike Samuel, so I shook my head and held up my hand to stay him, for though Samuel is weak he was raving so, I didn't know what harm he was fit to do. Thanks be to God Jimmy held back.

By that time, Samuel had drove me to a fury on account of myself as well as my children. I said my final piece and turned my back on him afore I could utter the blackest things filling my mouth, for 'twould have only enraged him further and dismayed my children all the more.

Though I sold them books for naught but love for my children, now the battle is done I'm scouring my conscience and am suffering a bit of the guilts. To give the devil his due, there was merit in Samuel's anger. Even afore himself took to raving at me, I'd begun to rue what I'd done for I knew what them books meant to him. Them things was all that was left to him of his Daddy.

'Tis a tizzy I'm in, for I confess I was in a bit of a snit when I traipsed down to Mr. Middleton's carrying them books under my oxter, for there was naught in the cupboard but the handful of flour and the odd jar of pickled pig's trotters and last fall's stewed apples. There was naught but two pennies in the jar, not nearly enough for to buy the milk and the eggs and the soup bones for to make a proper meal, 'specially for Samuel's lungs. Sorely troubled I was, for how could a good wife and mother put such a pittance on the table for her hungry brood? And I was fretting so about the coming cold and how the children have growed out their tattered clothes and shoes.

I shouldn't be after flogging myself so. I had the rightest purpose for selling them wore out books of his. I was caring for my family as best I could, looking out for himself as well as our babies. For Samuel to curse me and say them awful hurtful things was beyond spiteful. He showed me a vile side to himself I never knew was there. I can't look on him the same as afore, and I don't know what will become of us now. As a Catholic wife, 'tis my duty to mend this awful rift whether I will it or not, but I daren't approach him anytime soon, fey as he is.

'Tis a new turn, and frightful 'tis. The fury of him was beyond the beyond, though Samuel's changeable moods has always been a burden. Many's the time he's after being troubled with the melancholy broods when his face shuts itself and his blue eyes turn as gray and gloomy as rain clouds. He's far off and away, mired in a dismal place.

Other times, when his face gets to crumpling and the tears to dripping, 'tis clear he's gone completely astray in his wits. He starts up with the quaking and whimpering like a fretful baby. 'Tis shocking beyond measure to see a full-growed man display such shameful weakness.

Our first years together, I'd try to rouse him by talking or singing to him in the soothing voice I used on my own restive babies. When that did no good, I'd softly clout his face to bring him back to me. All for naught. I learnt 'twas best to leave him to himself those times and let him simmer down. I tell myself he's more to be pitied than scorned, for the muddling fright that shows on his face is piteous to behold.

But tonight, when he found I'd sold his books, he looked on me with such hatred, I quaked. His face was flushed and his eyes was popping out his head and his fists was clenched as if to do me harm. Threatening he was, and I was worried for my children, something I'd never thought would come to pass.

I fear Samuel might be a lunatic.

There's no reasoning with him now. No living with him whilst he's so enraged.

I'm of two minds, both gloomy as can be. We need to get back Samuel's books so's we can mend this rift between us, so's he'll not be after acting the crazy man. For without them books, I can't see him ever forgiving me and settling down. How can a family live in a house torn asunder by a lunatic?

But we can't be after using my laundress money to pay his brother back neither, as 'tis needed to keep us fed. And the pittance I earn means 'twould take most of a year to repay. Samuel can't be thinking right to beg off his brother like a common tinker! And all for some wore out books that don't do the rest of us no good at all. 'Tis shameful beyond words.

'Tis a pretty pass we've come to. I've been in dismal states afore, and there's nothing for it but to trust in God and the holy saints. I'll be on my knees at the prayers all the livelong night and leave tomorrow's unfolding in God's hands.

SAMUEL

Three days ago, I rose with the cockcrow and traipsed down the long road to Middleton's store. Coughing and wheezing in the cold November damp, I doubted I'd make it. But get there I did to find Middleton opening his doors for business. I introduced myself and I asked him in a most courteous way to hold my Daddy's books 'til I could buy them back on the Friday.

With barely a glance my way, he had the bollocks to say he'd already sold them -- though I could see those very books of which I spoke tidily arranged on the shelf behind his very self!

"What are you on about?" said I pointing to the selfsame books. "They're after sitting right there behind your very noggin."

"But they were bought and paid for just before I closed the shop last evening," he said, all twitchy and shifty-eyed. "The gentleman is picking them up later today."

I knew by his jittery demeanor that he was after lying, so I told him what they meant to me, how my Daddy treasured them and how I'd carried them with me across the sea all those years ago. But Middleton wouldn't budge, the lousy shite. He kept on asserting he'd already sold them and he couldn't back out the deal. In desperation, I offered to pay him five dollars so he'd profit by two over what he'd paid Julia, though I knew naught where I'd get such a tidy sum.

Middleton peered at me sharp-eyed as a vulture scrutinizing a carcass for freshness and asked, "If your missus bartered with me for the three dollars I paid, why should I believe you have five dollars to buy them back?"

"She didn't know what she was about, but I will have the money on the Friday," I said.

"But I've already told you, it's too late. I've sold them to a gentleman for a tidy profit."

"And what did this gentleman pay?"

"More than you've got I'll warrant." His beady eyes gleamed.

"I'll match his price," said I, knowing 'twasn't much truth in it but desperate was I beyond reason.

He stared at me, and I could see the calculations going on inside his greedy head. "Alright," said he, "you come back on Friday with nine dollars and I'll sell them all back to you." His rapacious eyes showed not a jot of shame for his previous lie.

Tempted I was to ask what he'd tell his 'buyer' when he returned his payment to him, but fearful of the shite changing his mind I said, "I'll see you on Friday."

I hobbled back home, fretting the entire way. Damn that stony-hearted Middleton for his greediness! Demanding three times what he paid for them not two days prior? From a desperate and sickly man? How was I to borrow nine dollars from William? Three was bad enough, but at least 'twas possible.

So these past three days I've been sorely distraught, trying to get up the courage to ask such a tidy sum from William. If he has it to hand, he'd give it to me, for he alone knows how precious are our Daddy's books. But 'tis overmuch for a man with a family in his care to part with, especially when we both know I'll naught be able to repay him. Worse still, 'twould shame me beyond the beyond to beg for the money as I'd have to confess that my own wife went behind my back. Surely William's Lydia would never betray him like that.

And now 'tis Friday, and since the nine dollars have not fallen from the heavens, I've not got the means to buy my own precious books back. I'm sick to death at the thought of someone else's unworthy hands touching them. A pox on that greedy whoreson Middleton, that shite-faced liar. The curse of Cromwell be on him and all his progeny for all eternity. I hope I'll not ever have to look on his despicable self again, for surely I would murder him.

Since her perfidy is what began this woeful state of affairs, I cannot look on that vile Julia, can barely abide being in the same room with her let alone sleep beside her. I've taken to sleeping in the chair by the fire, though 'tis causing a terrible stiffness and swelling in my legs and cricks in my neck and back. But put up with it I will since that pernicious woman is the heartscald to me.

Those books served as talismans betokening my happy childhood before The Hunger and all the woes that followed. Without the consolation of Daddy's books, my wits have gone further astray. I'm broken into tiny bits that won't ever fit back together, more wrecked than I was after that calamitous Gettysburg.

Too exhausted am I to crawl out this blackest pit of sickness and despair. And to what purpose? To be nursed by an aggrieved wife when the two of us can't abide to look on one another? I'll never be anywhere near to being whole, to being of any worth to myself or my children. There's nothing for it but for me to go. I must take myself out of this life.

Arrah, I'll miss the children for sure, especially my sweet Sarah. But 'tisn't decent for them to be seeing their Mammy and Daddy at the battling all the livelong day and night, or flouting one another in stony silence.

'Tis come to a sorry pass when your own children fear you, but there you have it. Since the Monday evening when I lost my temper so sorely, they look on me like wary wee animals waiting for me to pounce. It pains and shames me. My littlest Maggie hasn't come to me these past few mornings to sit on my knee as she's accustomed to doing, but keeps away and stares at me from behind her Mammy's skirts with her big green eyes full of fear. This morning, I smiled as big as I could and bid her to sit, but she turned from me and hid.

Yesterday, Denny who's but five pulled himself up tall like a man defending his own and peered at me and asked, "Why do you hate my Ma so?" His face was fluxing grief and outrage.

I glanced at Julia who turned her stiff back to me as if to remove herself from the discussion. I turned back to Denny and spluttered, "I don't hate your Mammy."

"You screamed at her and called her mean names," he said his voice cracking. "And you're after giving her the black looks all the time."

"Arrah boyo, 'tis sick I am, not angry," I prevaricated. "The consumption makes me bad-tempered, and I'm heartily sorry for it."

"If you ever hurt my Ma," said my own dear boy, his wee face menacing, "I will murder you."

Astounded I was at the anger in his eyes, and wounded sore to the quick. "Jesus Mary and Joseph lad, why would you be after thinking I'd do your mammy harm?"

"Because you were so fiercely mad, like a big mean bear. You looked like you would clout her."

Then dear Sarah, who'd been wiping the breakfast dishes, said in her placating way, "Hush Denny! You know Pa would never hurt a one of us." Then she looked on me as if to assure herself of the veracity of her statement.

"For the love of God," I fairly shouted, "Of course I wouldn't! For love you all I do."

"'Cepting Ma," said Denny as he turned from me.

Stricken I was by those jarring words. Yet, I dared not look on Julia for fear the truth would out.

Eamon had been watching the entire scene in silence and peered at me in a most doubtful way with eyes much older than his seven years.

Maggie continued to hide behind her Mammy's skirts.

It shames me terribly, my shattering of my family's trust. Yet I don't know how to remedy it. I haven't the will to forgive Julia for her betrayal, can't even look on her. She knows she's done wrong, yet is stony cold toward me and says naught a word. There's naught but ice between us, and I can't see that 'twill ever thaw.

My mind is made up. I'll be off and down the riverside with the sharpened razor before dawn. I can't abide one more day being a sickly, useless burden; looked upon by my children as an odious brute; being constantly reminded of my insufficiencies by that deceitful, cold-hearted woman.

My being gone for good would be better for the children all-around. I won't be after burdening them with my uselessness and my angry bellowing and my straying wits. There'll be none of the battling that terrifies them so, that makes them fear their very own Daddy.

They'll not lose a thing in my passing, only gain, for 'twill be one less mouth to feed and no doctor's fees. Yes, they will fare better without me. For Poulson assured me that widows and orphans get a plenteous share in a soldier's pension. That, along with Julia's laundress pennies will make things right as rain.

JULIA

When I woke this morning to make the tea and biscuits, I found the chair aside the fire empty. 'Tis where Samuel's been sleeping these last few nights as he's become such the madman, he won't come near me at all. Himself was nowhere about, so I thought he'd gone down the jakes.

A half hour passed and he hadn't come back and I was getting twitchy. He was never a one to linger in the jakes, was always a one to get his business done in a hurry, especially if 'twas cold.

By now the children was all awake, and Sarah asked after her Pa. Though but nine, she's old in mind and sensed something amiss. Her eyes was big with worry.

"He's down the jakes, no doubt," said I with as much calmness as I could muster. "Youse all eat your biscuits now, whilst I go see if himself needs help with the stairs."

"I'll go with you Ma," Sarah said as she scarpered toward the door.

"No youse won't. I can see to him myself. Youse will stay here and look after the others."

I banged the door shut behind me to hinder any protests, then run down the steps, fretting the whole way. When I got to the jakes, I saw the door ajar and yanked it fully open, fearing to find himself dead on the seat. But he wasn't there, wasn't nowhere in the yard. I went around front and peered all down the street, but 'twas only the milkman I found driving his cart.

Angry as I was at himself for being so devilishly lunatic towards me, my heart took to thrashing with worry. Where could he be at this hour? And in this November cold and damp. How long had he been gone? He'd been in such a angry brood all week long there was no telling what he'd gone off and done. But the state of him was so poorly, he couldn't have gone far.

I slowly climbed back up the stairs, pondering what I should do and what I'd tell the children. When I reached the landing, there was Sarah wringing her hands.

"Where's Pa?" Near to tears she was, and had the knowing look in her eye.

"I don't know," was all I could muster.

"He's run off, hasn't he?"

"Did youse not hear me? I said I don't know!"

"Where else could Pa be but gone away from us? Just like Mr. Scanlon!"

Her pinched face was full of worry. Our downstairs neighbor Mr. Scanlon had gallivanted off on a bright Sunday afternoon never to return, leaving his poor missus with a hungry brood of seven to be looking after. And then there was Mr. O'Toole a few doors down, forever gone in his cups, who'd gone off last year, abandoning his brood of six. 'Tis the curse of the Irish women, their fainthearted men running off on them like that. I couldn't look on Sarah, but replied with my fondest hope.

"Maybe he's just gone down the road somewheres on his own to straighten his wits some for to be in a better state when he comes back."

"But Ma," she said, her lip a-quivering, "he can't hardly go down the stairs before he takes to wheezing and coughing and failing in the knees! How could he go down the road?"

Pitiful she looked, but my nerves was all frayed and overtook me.

"Oh child, quit your nattering and see to the little ones!"

"Pa's gone, and it's your fault!" she shouted of a sudden. "You sold his Daddy's books, and he's naught been right since." The saucy look of her was beyond brazen.

"Youse little snit!" I cried as I clouted her cheek. "Youse shut that bold mouth of yours and get inside afore all the neighbors hear." I thrust her toward the door, but she turned on me.

"You chased Pa away!" She bellowed, then stood there staring up at me, her fierce blue eyes leaking tears and her gob all pursed in a pout, something I can't never abide.

"I could put a stove on that lip of yours! Now youse stop that pouting and sassing, and get inside."

"I'm going to find Pa!"

"My foot youse are! You'll be after minding me!"

Quick as a wink, that child ducked around me and scarpered off down the stairs. I took after her, but that wee thing was gone in a trice, and without her coat in this harsh weather!

Now 'tis nearing noon, and I've got the husband and the daughter lost from the house, and I'm beyond the beyond with vexation and worry. Mary and Jimmy have been out searching hither, thither, and yon these past four hours.

Mostly I'm fretting on account of Sarah, for she's out in the cold damp scouring them streets wearing nothing but that thin worn frock. She'll be after catching her death. She'll pay it no mind as she's a mulish little thing 'specially when it comes to her Pa who can't do no wrong in her eyes, even though that rascal run out on the lot of us without nary a care for her feelings. He don't deserve such devotion.

Worse yet, my poor lamb is astray in this city and some of them streets and alleyways is unsavory with the drunkards and lousers of all kinds, and she's such a wee thing, barely nine years old. Beyond worried I am for her safety. And 'tis all on account of that rapscallion of a husband, that foulest of fathers. I never thought he'd be after doing such a dirty deed.

If my Sarah don't come home, if Mary and Jimmy can't find her, I don't know what I'll do. And if they're after finding Samuel and bringing him back instead, I'll be after giving that louser a piece of my mind for putting our daughter in peril.

Mother of God, I pray my baby girl comes home safe.

SAMUEL

'Twas but four this morning when I rose and grabbed my sharpened razor and stowed it in my pocket. I crept up to my sleeping children nestled like a litter of puppies in their bed and softly kissed each of them in turn, mindful not to wake them. Sarah, being the light sleeper she is, stirred and opened her eyes.

"Pa," she mumbled, "is it time to get up?"

"No *mavourneen*," I whispered so as not to disturb the others, "I simply want to tell you I love you." My heart was squeezing with the hurt of leaving, for I knew I'd never see her dear little face again.

"I love you too, Pa," she whispered, regarding me quizzically. "Why are you up and about in the cold? Are you after feeling poorly?"

"No Dearie, I'm grand. I didn't mean to disrupt your sleep. Close your peepers and dream of lovely things."

"Yes, Pa." She regarded me with a fearful eye, for she was always after knowing my deepest heart thoughts, so I forced a smile and patted her head though I was near to tears. Soon she closed her eyes, and off I went.

'Twas a sad walk down the river, as I pondered the loss of my children. I barely felt the chill wind as I recalled their dear faces and the lilt of their voices as the scenes played over and over like a beloved song in my heart.

In due course, I found myself the perfect spot to die, where no one but the odd stranger or vigilant copper plodding along his daily watch would find me and likely not 'til the dead smell took to wafting off of me. 'Twas a wee alley back of a warehouse full of the cast-off barrels and crates. I wriggled my way in and found a cleared spot, sat myself down, and leaned against the brick wall. 'Twas cold, but leastways I was out the wind.

Biding my time, I contemplated the past, toting up my sins and regrets, weighing them against my hardships and upright deeds. In balance, 'twas not much gaiety to recall aside from the days before Mammy and Daddy died, and the odd times with William, and of course Ezra along with our boon comrades before the savage fighting commenced. And then the tender times with my children. I didn't let my heart ponder on Julia, for 'twas too aching a place to go.

My mind was astonishingly clear, and although I wasn't at all sure God existed, or if He did, in a form I was wont to understand, I elucidated my thoughts to Him. Though the pompous priests would refuse me a Requiem Mass and a burial plot in holy ground, decreeing that the doing away of myself was a mortal sin which damned me for all eternity to the pains of hellfire, I couldn't envision it being any the worse than the agony I was even now after suffering in body and mind. More significantly, my absence would be of great service to my family, so in all fairness God was wont to take that into the final accounting. If punishment was warranted, surely it would simply be the odd time in that dubious place called Purgatory.

My mind at ease, I settled in to do the deed. At least a dozen times I grasped the razor and placed it upon my throat just 'neath my ear, where the pulse is robust. But though the razor was beyond sharp and would do the job quite handily causing little pain, something there was that stayed my hand.

'Twas Sarah's worried face kept coming back to me and her fretful voice inquiring: "Why are you up and about in the cold?" Though I strove mightily to overcome this unsolicited visitation, I could not flout that dear face nor sink that cold blade into my flesh.

Exasperated, I reminded myself of all the weighty reasons for ending my life: my feebleness and pain; my befuddlement and strayed wits; my children's dread of me; Julia's betrayal; her constant reproach which rendered me unmanned; the loss of Daddy's books; my inability to support my own sorry self nor my family. My utter futility.

For wasn't I already a dying husk of a man? 'Twas cruel to let my children witness their Daddy wasting away and surviving to do naught but battle with their Mammy. They'd never known me when I was hale and hearty, when my wits were sharp and clear, when I was a cheery, affable fellow. Nigh on fifteen years the consumption has been battering my lungs, encumbering my heart, murdering me by degrees. These last months have been worse by far with the fevers and the coughing up the great gouts of blood, and I'll never be at the work again. 'Tis near to death I am anyway, so 'tis no reason not to hasten it along.

Thus did I spend this morning ruminating in a contradictory state until I heard the church bells tolling nine. I had tarried in that alley for nigh on three hours, and I was still alive! Beyond angry I was at myself, and with newfound resolve I lifted the razor to my throat. But my hand was so benumbed by the cold that I couldn't grasp it properly, and it slipped through my fingers.

Fearful of making a painful, fruitless mess of it, I laid the razor aside. I blew on my hands, rubbed them together, then stove them 'neath my oxters to warm them up. My backside was numb from sitting on the cold ground, and my feet were prickling with the pins and needles. I thought if I stood and paced a bit, I could get my blood moving again. But when I tried to stand, I had the giving out of my legs. In my struggle to right myself, I grabbed a barrel just beside me and didn't it go tumbling and rolling so I fell flat on my arse in the same spot from whence I'd started.

I sat there for a bit, stirring my legs to and fro to get them working. Then I leaned back, braced my hands against the brick wall of the warehouse, and with utmost difficulty, pushed myself up to standing. That exertion bushwhacked my plans, for I started in with the fit of coughing and wheezing and panting. Such a racket I made that a fellah heard me and hollered down the alleyway, "Who's there?"

I couldn't utter a word what with the coughing and gasping, and I heard him making his way toward me, shoving the barrels and crates aside.

"Oy vey!" he said, peering at me with eyes as big as saucers. "What are you doing back here? You look near to death."

I felt the bloody drool dripping off my chin, and I swiped it away with my sleeve. I tried to speak, but couldn't for lack of air as well as answer.

"Come with me man, in out of the cold." He came toward me and grabbed ahold of my arm. Though shorter than myself, his grasp was firm as a vise. Stout as a barrel he was, but his black eyes were soft with pity.

Like a biddable child I let him guide me inside the warehouse where he led me to a hearty fire roaring away inside a metal barrel. Beyond grateful I was for the warmth as he positioned me opposite the smoky side where I held my hands forth to thaw.

We stood there assessing one another for a time whilst my coughing settled and my wheezing eased up. 'Twas then I noticed he wore one of those wee round caps atop his head, the sort the Jews wear, and I wondered how it stayed in place on that bald pate of his.

Putting his hand forth he said, "I am Gabe Singer. I manage this establishment."

Lamely, I returned his handshake for my crippled right hand was throbbing something fierce as it began to thaw and come back to life.

"Samuel I am," I uttered through gasps, "and grateful beyond words for the fire."

He nodded as if to say 'twas nothing whilst he frankly perused the state of me. "If you don't mind me saying Samuel, you're an ailing man, certainly not fit to be out in this cold." His black eyes held mine. "Why were you back there? Were you seeking shelter?"

His keen eyes, though perceptive, were kind, and as I was too weary and miserable to tell fables I answered his questions without prevarication.

"I do have a home, but I left for reasons I'd rather keep to myself."

"I see," he stroked his bearded chin. "Haven't you anywhere else to go? No kin or acquaintances?"

"I've a friend away across the river in Gloucester City and I've a brother in Manayunk, but I won't be after burdening either one for they have their own families to care for."

"But surely a brother wouldn't want you suffering alone in this raw weather. Especially ailing as you are."

I looked away from those sympathetic eyes. "I'll be alright," I mumbled "once I'm warmed up."

"You need a sight more than warming up, Samuel. You need a physician. I can have my nephew take you over . . ."

"The doctors can't do any more for me. I'm dying of the consumption and there's naught that can be done."

"Well then, it seems your brother would undeniably want to be caring for you in your mortal state. Was it Manayunk you say he lives? I can spare a man the time to drive you over there in a wagon."

I hesitated, and he yelled, "Aaron!"

A young man appeared. "Yes, Uncle Gabe?"

"This is my friend Samuel who needs immediate conveyance to Manayunk. Leave off your loading, and hitch that wagon there and take him, please."

"Yes Uncle," Aaron said, then tended to the wagon as he was bid.

Gabe turned to me, "You're still trembling with the cold. Would you like tea or coffee for the trip?"

"Tea would be lovely, thank you."

By the time Gabe returned with the tea – piping hot and enhanced with a dollop of milk and a spot of sugar -- as well as a thick slab of buttered bread, Aaron was ready with the wagon. He assisted me up into the seat and wrapped a heavy woolen horse blanket around my shoulders and draped another one over my lap.

Gabe handed me the plate of bread and the cup of steaming brew. "Best of luck to you, Samuel."

Gratefully, I set the plate on my lap and wrapped my stiff hands around the hot cup.

"A thousand thank yous for your kindness, Gabe," was all I could muster -- such a paltry reward for that kindest of men.

Aaron must have sensed my fretful state for he left me to my thoughts, saying naught a word as he drove me all the way across that vast city to Manayunk. For those two hours, I agonized about what I would tell William. Though I'd never admit to my initial intention of doing away with myself, how would I explain my leaving Julia and the children? How could William comprehend my situation? And Lydia his wife, so kind and caring, how would she ever understand? For how could either one of them, happy and hale as they are, see it in any other light than me abandoning my own brood?

JULIA

Thanks be to God, Jimmy brought my Sarah home safe last night, though she traipsed them cold streets the livelong day searching for her shiftless Pa. 'Twas nigh on dusk when them two trudged up the stairs, her wee self a-shivering and her face so drawn and sad. I heard their foot-treads and ran out on the landing to pull her inside to warm and feed the poor frozen thing.

So relieved was I to set eyes on her that I couldn't scold her for running off like that, though I did tell her this morning how sorely grieved I was at her naughtiness in not minding me and the awful hours I spent fretting for herself.

Though my darling boyo Jimmy went back out and searched well past dark, he couldn't find no trace of Samuel. Didn't my poor wee Sarah cry herself to sleep. I heard her sobbing the livelong night, but I left her to herself as there was naught I could do to comfort her.

As for that scoundrel of a husband who put my poor lamb into such a state of peril and grief, I'm nearly past caring what he's done with his lousy self. 'Tis mostly for Sarah's sake that I want him accounted for. I can't think where he could have gallivanted off to other than to his brother's house somewheres over in Manayunk-- the self-same brother who he was going to write to beg for the money to get his books back.

I barely know the man nor his wife, for the brothers don't see each other no more due to the distance – it takes forever and a day to get there – so 'tis just the letter writing they do. They was once thick as thieves. Samuel lived with William and his family afore the war, so 'tis likely they would take him in. And they're welcome to him.

If Samuel has any concern for his children, he'll surely send them a note. 'Twould put poor Sarah's mind to rest if she knew he was safe.

Peculiar thing is, Samuel's razor is gone from its customary spot aside the washbasin, but his comb and toothbrush is still setting there. Why would he care about the shaving, but leave off the rest? Worse still, he left his opium drops setting there aside the teapot, the opium being the only remedy for his cough. And he never touched the few pennies in the jar, but left them be.

I can't fathom it. A man who can barely walk without the giving out of his legs, feeble with the gasping and the coughing, sallies forth afore dawn with no money, no medicine, with naught but a razor in his pocket.

I suppose it could be for to defend himself against the ruffians that skulk about the riverside and alleyways. But still, to leave everything else behind that he needs for his basic comfort?

Mother of God! What if he was after taking that razor to cause himself harm? For as sick and broody and lunatic as he's been lately, I can't help but think maybe he wandered off somewheres private to do away with himself. 'Twould send his soul directly to Hell! I'd not wish that fate on the vilest of Englishmen. Certainly not my own husband, vexing though he be.

If he be pondering such a thing, 'twould lay a heavy burden on my soul. For surely, I was colder to him than I ought to have been, nattering at him when I should have shut my gob, selling them books in a snit. If I've driven him to his death, I will have an equal share in God's punishment. Now that is affrighting me something fierce and giving me the guilts.

But aren't I imagining the worst of things when most likely 'tis the least? He's likely just in a sulk and gallivanted off somewheres and will be back when he's settled some.

I'll pull out my beads now, be at the rosary storming heaven for Samuel not to do something rash. And I'll be asking for forgiveness for the two of us for all of our angry bickering.

Presently I must put on the hopeful face for Sarah's sake. If Samuel's not back by tomorrow morn, I'll send Jimmy down the police station to see if they've any news, and to ask them to keep a lookout.

Jesus Mary and Joseph, what a vexing man I married!

SAMUEL

So nimbly did the lie fall from my lips that I half believed it myself.

"Julia has left me and taken the children across the river to New Jersey. She wouldn't tell me where, just swore the children would be safe."

William, his wife Lydia, and myself were sitting in his parlor, me imbibing my second glass of warmed whiskey. Though lying to my own brother and bearing such malign false witness against Julia lay heavy on my conscience, 'twas the only way I could think to justify my leaving my children whilst also keeping my brother from communicating with Julia. I had to make him believe Julia and the children were unreachable. 'Twas a sharp edge I was treading, indeed.

"I can't believe Julia would deprive you of the comfort of your own children," said Lydia. She was sore perturbed. "Certainly, she'll come back after she's cooled some."

"Julia was angrier than I've ever seen her. She accused me of being an unfit father, not caring enough to provide for my children, not doing my utmost to earn a wage."

"But surely," said Lydia her eyes soft with concern, "she can see how grievously ill you are."

"Sure, 'tis clear as can be, but she won't accept it." Weaving truth with fancy, I further elucidated. "Ashamed I am to admit to you that my step-children were keeping us fed in Gloucester City where Franky and Mary worked down the mill. That's why I wanted to come back here, where I thought I'd find the work to do the supporting. But all for naught. Now they're all gone across the river to who knows what parts, and I can't stay in the boarding house for I can't be after paying the landlord and feeding myself on my paltry two dollar a month pension. So here I am, and sorry to be dumping my disgraceful self on your doorstep. Mortified I am to be burdening you, but I hope my two dollars a month will help defray my room and board."

"Arrah, none of that," William waved it off. "You know you can stay here as long as you need. But first we should have Doc Brewster take a look on you."

"Don't be after bothering. The surgeons have all given up on me. My worn-out lungs are past saving."

Ashamed I am to say that my mendacity was believed by those two innocent souls without question. Living a lie is weighing heavy on my conscience, yet I can't find any way around it.

Thus, here I am two months later still living at my brother's house on his sufferance as well as his dear wife's. Lydia daily holds the high hopes of me reuniting with my family. When she asked if I had left William's address with my landlord at my former boarding house, I assured her I had, the lie sticking like a lump of acrid dough in my gullet.

This morning, William took me all the way over to Front Street to see attorney Poulson to try once more to get a larger pension. 'Twas William's idea, for when I offered him the two dollars a month for my upkeep, he refused it and said for me to save it for when I am reunited with Julia and the children.

"Very likely, she'll have second thoughts and return home," he said, all innocence itself. "Or the children will clamor for their daddy. Is your former landlord trustworthy to provide Julia with my address?"

"That he is," I lied yet once again. "He knows how imperative 'tis. Herself will contact me if she wants to."

So steeped was I in my web of lies it shamed me no end. Yet I could not have William doing some well-intentioned investigating only to find out 'twas all a reprehensible tale I'd told him. 'Tis true what my Daddy always told us. Lying is a vile sin as one leads to another and 'tis hard to keep them all straight.

Sure enough, my tale was close to unravelling as we came upon Race Street on our way to Poulson's. For William knew my post office address from our earlier correspondence. Since the war, we had regularly exchanged letters as we lived too far apart to be visiting one another.

So, weren't we just two blocks from my erstwhile abode where for all I knew Julia still resided when he asked, "'Tis round about here you lived wasn't it? On this very street?"

Fortunately, Race Street is a lengthy thoroughfare which aided me in my equivocation.

"Not too far from here," I said in a vague way, pulling my hat down lower upon my brow and wrapping the scarf up around my snout, acting as though 'twas against the bitter January wind when 'twas because I was fretting I'd be espied by Julia or one of the children, or a prying neighbor.

"Tell me where," said William, "and we'll stop and check with the landlord. See if Julia's left you any message."

His soft amber eyes looked on me with such guileless care that I cast my own eyes away and down the road. Mother of God, I couldn't be after giving him the precise house number, for 'twould expose me for the deceitful louser I was.

"Ah sure," I pointed in the opposite direction along Race Street, "'tis just a few blocks down."

As we arrived at a fairly safe distance from my former domicile, I searched for a likely boarding house where I could continue my pretense.

"There 'tis, just over there. Now you stay with the horse and buggy whilst I go in."

Soon as we halted, I fairly jumped down from the cart to waylay William accompanying me. Fortuitously, I found the door unbolted and rushed inside. My haste cost me dearly for I struggled for breath and had to lean against the wall inside the entryway. But pleased I was to find no one about. I tarried for a few minutes, then back out the door to my waiting brother.

"He's heard not a word," said I, putting on my most downcast look as I sat down beside him.

"Give her some time," William said, patting my knee. "She's sure to come around."

"Meantime, let's be off!" I said as I hunkered in the seat, making myself as imperceptible as possible. "'Tis colder than a monk's wick out here!"

In short order we arrived at Poulson's office on Front Street. Upon seeing my fevered face and hearing my raucous rales, Poulson's demeanor reflected his certainty that I was not long for this world. He said he'd try once more for an increase in my disability, but didn't hold out much hope. The government wasn't after being any more generous than 'twas before and would likely rule again that my consumption was not the army's liability.

He seemed not a jot surprised at my separation from Julia and the children. He said he'd heard this tale of woe countless times and, much to my relief, didn't request details.

As I watched him speak, I couldn't help but ponder once again upon what a peculiar looking fella he was with those faded blue eyes of his all bugged out like a frog -- like marbles ready to roll right off his face. Chinless as he was with those bugged out eyes, I realized with a start that he bore a striking resemblance to the vile Famine Queen! Yet, I swore I would not hold that against him, for he was doing his utmost to aid me.

Afterwards, William took me to a tavern. He requested a fireside table, and we dined on steaming beef stew, mopping up the rich gravy with sourdough bread. Surprised I was at my ravenous appetite, and I ate with gusto. My brother was so pleased that he ordered us hot whiskey which braced us for the long, cold drive back to Manayunk.

JULIA

I've not seen hide nor hair of that scoundrel Samuel for nine months. That first month, I fretted so, for I couldn't get it out my head that he'd done away with himself. The police was never after finding him, though I suspect they didn't look too hard, him being an Irisher. For they suspect all Irishers of being lost to the drink and absconding on their families which, more's the pity, is too often the truth of it.

Jimmy read the newspapers every day for a full month checking to see if a body was found, but none showed up. Yet I fretted every day. What if he ended up in the river? So addled that he fell in or leapt in? Or found some hidey-hole to crawl into and used that razor of his? God forgive him if he did.

Then lo and behold, the following month didn't his pension payment not arrive at our Post Office. That's when I knew the rapscallion must be alive and having them sent elsewheres. 'Tis clear he didn't do away with himself after all, which is a small mercy as it relieves my conscience. So now 'tis full rage I'm feeling toward him. How he could go galivanting off, leaving me and our wee children to fend for ourselves is beyond the beyond, though many an Irishman does just that. 'Tis a curse on our race of men to be so weak and shiftless. My Pa was the exception, but 'tis the Irish women has all the strength of mind and character.

The blame is partly my own for lack of judgement. Samuel was always fey, even when first we met, but I paid it little mind as I didn't know the depth of his melancholy. 'Twasn't 'til after we was wed that I realized 'twasn't in the clouds where his head was. No, that man's mind was in a dark place. A sad place. A bitter place. And now himself has left it to myself to provide for his own blooded children.

So's that's why we're living back here in Gloucester City. Without Samuel's pension we couldn't make ends meet in that boarding house in Philadelphia where I never wished to go in the first place. But Samuel, in his fevered mind, insisted 'twould ensure him the employ on the docks. Jesus Mary and Joseph, I should never have given into his foolish whim.

I had been yearning the whole time to go back home to Gloucester City where my Franky and my brother Daniel live. So 'twasn't a hard decision. But Sarah, who lives on the daily hope that her villainous Pa will return, nearly lost her wits, crying that her Pa would never be able to find us. So before I took ourselves back, I had her write a note to leave with the landlord telling where Samuel could be after finding us if the louser ever turns up. I haven't heard nothing so far.

I've got us three lovely rooms in a tidy boarding house on Cumberland Street down the road from my old church, St. Mary's. 'Tis Father Halloran I have to thank for arranging it. For 'tis his kindly cousin who owns the boarding house, and he's after charging me a most fair price and willing to wait the extra day or two if needed for to make the payment. Ashamed I was to have to be telling Father my tale of woe, but of course he'd be after knowing it anyway since priests can see into our very souls, 'specially to the most shameful secrets. 'Tis some kind of holy magic they have.

My brother Daniel would be only too delighted to help me, but I won't be after taking advantage of his generosity as 'tis only myself I have to blame for being in this predicament. 'Twas me who chose to wed Samuel with them weak lungs of his and them straying wits, and with my fruitful womb I was just asking for trouble.

Thanks be to God, my Mary who is nineteen got her job back at the gingham mill, only this time she's in the dyehouse where her lungs isn't bothered by the lint. Jimmy got himself a job in the spinning room, and the two of them are earning enough for the seven of us to eke by.

But worried I am for my Jimmy as the lint is after troubling his lungs just like it bothered Mary's afore. He's got a wheeze on him, and I fear his chest can't take the work much longer. The dyehouse don't need no more workers so there's no help for him there. But though just fifteen, he's my cleverest child, and he let the overseer know that he's right good with the ciphering and can help with keeping the ledgers. The overseer said he would pass that on to the manager.

If 'tweren't for my Mary and my Jimmy, the wolf would be at our very door, for starving we'd be. And I don't use that word at all lightly, for as I told you afore, I suffered through *an Gorta Mor* in Ireland when I was just a wee girl. I know what starvation is. And I won't stand for my children to suffer it.

My poor Kate is an innocent – her wits is slow, so she's always behind like the tail of the cow, never paying no mind to what she's about. She's sixteen, and when she saw her younger brother Jimmy join Mary down the mill, she said to me, "Mammy, when will I be going down the mill?"

Her freckly face, so sweet, broke my heart for I couldn't tell her the truth – that she's too slow in the wits, that she wouldn't be able to keep up, that they'd surely send her on her way after the first day or two. Worse still, I'd not trust her to keep herself safe. The mill's a dangerous place for a one like her who's in foggy dew land all the live long day. I could see Kate a-woolgathering whilst her hair came unbound and caught itself in the bobbin and her scalp came a-ripping clear off her head. That very thing happened a couple of years back to a wee girl working right aside Mary, and 'twas dreadful for she nearly bled to death and now has the half-bald head to show for it. And then there's the danger with the fingers getting too close to the cutter and slicing one or two clear off.

I couldn't tell my sweet Kate that, so I said, "Dearie, youse is needed here to help with the young ones. I need the extra eyes to watch after Denny and Maggie." And I smiled at her as I lied, for in truth she's more the hindrance than the help, but she's sweet as the day is long. And that darling girl believed me and was soothed.

Sarah is nigh on ten, but old for her years. Always was. She loves nothing more than the book learning, so she won't be happy when I pull her out of school next year and send her to join Mary and Jimmy down the mill.

The others are still little: Eamon is eight, Denny is six, and little Maggie is but four. Ah, my prettiest child Maggie is such a fretful wee thing, her loveliness being all on the outside. Prickly and whiny, she's also after being melancholy like her sister Sarah. More's the pity, they both take after their Pa that way.

As for Samuel, I've pondered on his leaving through all these past months and I am well and truly stymied. He could've gadded off to his brother's somewheres in Manayunk, a place I've never been. He'd no other place to go. His oldest friend Michael Killian lives here in Gloucester City, and I'm well acquainted with him for 'twas him who witnessed our marriage. I saw Michael at Mass the one Sunday, and when I told him how Samuel up and left us, he was well and truly astonied.

The thing is, so sick was Samuel when he absconded, I wonder if he still be alive all these months later. His consumption was tearing him to bits, what with the fevered spots on his cheeks and his body thinning out. And he was after coughing up the great gouts of fresh blood.

Broken as he was in body and mind, lunatic as he was when I sold them books of his, I wonder was himself so muddled in the head that he didn't know what he was about when he traipsed off. Just walked on down the road searching for somewheres he belonged. Ended up who knows where. And I wonder was it him or someone else who told the government to stop sending them pension checks to our post office.

I'm sorely troubled by these thoughts as I don't like to think he's suffering overmuch or that 'twas me that sent a dying man off with my nattering.

Yet I can't say I miss him, for living with that man was a trial. He was always after having the nightmares even during the day. You'd think he was back there in battle what with his hollering and twitching and sweating. And then he'd take to weeping, the tears falling so fast they was dripping off his face. 'Twas altogether shameful to behold.

What sort of man does that?

SAMUEL

I arrived here in Dayton in the back of beyond at The Soldiers' Home last month, on August twentieth in the year of our Lord eighteen-seventy-eight.

In the nine months I abided with William, my lungs and heart declined so severely and my melancholy grew so deep that I lost my appetite and spent most of my days abed. Poor Lydia was always after trying to tempt me with the stews and the soups and the fresh baked bread, but 'twas all for naught. I grew weaker each day, and 'twas clear I was near to dying.

Aside from my debilities, I was after suffering the guilts for having been unable to live up to my domestic as well as soldiering duties. Most especially for the wicked lie I had told about Julia, though for the children's sake I had no choice. Yet such weakness is insufferable and unpardonable in a man.

How is it that a useless, ailing man longing for death remains alive for so long whilst a hale, hardworking man such as Julia's first husband drops dead out the blue? 'Tis an unjustifiable mystery.

'Twas way back in May on my last visit to see attorney Poulson, that he advised me about The Soldiers' Home. I'd kept up the lie about my wife deserting me and running off across the river to parts unknown in New Jersey, and me having no one left in the world to tend me but my brother, which made me eligible for consideration. I think Poulson was after feeling the guilts that he hadn't been able to get me a raise in my pension. Though in all fairness, I don't think 'twas his fault at all.

He'd written to me to visit him so he could impart the details. William carted me to his office on Front Street and sat by my side as Poulson explained his findings. 'Twas clear he was shaken at my appearance, what with my thinning out and my sallow skin and my choking cough that was bringing up ever more freshets of blood. He looked on me, his watery frog eyes more sympathetic than I'd ever seen them.

"One of my colleagues travelled to Dayton to see for himself," Poulson said, tapping the folder on his desk. "He was highly impressed, said it's a top-notch facility they're operating out there in

Ohio. The Soldiers' Home employs only the most skilled surgeons who provide the best, up-to-date care."

He opened the folder, pulled out a map and slid it across the desk for William and myself to peruse.

"As you can see, the grounds are structured like a town separate from the hospital. Instead of wards, the veterans live in dormitories and have access to acres of open land with walkways, gardens, and a chapel providing Protestant and Catholic services."

Here he leaned in and smiled for the first time ever before continuing, "Best of all Samuel, you wouldn't have to worry about relying on your pension money or your brother's generosity anymore since room and board and medical care are all free of charge to our Union veterans. There is a waiting period, but since you are faring so poorly, I can register you as a priority case. I'd be only too happy to complete the paperwork."

So Poulson did, and 'twas but three months before I was accepted.

William and I stood on the station platform awaiting my train to Dayton. He clutched my satchel of meager belongings and mopped his brow in the August heat whilst I shivered with fever chills. Lost in our melancholy thoughts we said little, but 'twas clear he grieved our separation as much as I. When the train pulled in, we embraced, clutching one another tightly and near to weeping with the sorrow for we both knew 'twas our final parting.

William handed me my satchel, and after one last loving look to seal his beloved face forever in my mind and heart, I boarded the train. I took a seat on the far side of the car as I could not bear to look out the window at my brother and watch his stricken face recede as I waved goodbye.

Throughout a day and a night, I road that train six-hundred miles west. Whilst we tarried at several stations along the way to take on and disgorge passengers, we raced right on past others. And though I tried to appreciate the everchanging scenery, the rocking of the train, far from soothing me, only rekindled raw reminiscences of the medical train I'd ridden from Gettysburg to Cuyler. It troubled me something fierce to ponder the wastage of my last fifteen years since that hellacious ride. So deeply melancholic was I that I barely took note of the forests and mountains and fields and towns we traversed before ending up here in the back of beyond in the western edge of Ohio.

The first thing the authorities did upon my arrival was query me about my family relations. Considering I didn't want them finding Julia, I simplified things by stating I was a widower. Abashed I am to say that it gratified me some to imagine her deceased -- for then I would be shut of her altogether. Shut of her along with the guilt we two shared in the breakdown of our melancholy union.

Conversely, 'twas with the heaviest of hearts that I denied my children's existence, for I'd not disown my own blood under any but these most compulsory of circumstances. In my deepest heart I knew that them being rid of their burdensome Daddy was only to their good. 'Twas my brother's name I supplied as next of kin.

What happened next was a surprise. They sat me upon a stool in front of a black curtain. Facing me was a fella behind a camera.

"Arrah," I said. "Are you going to take a picture of my homely self?"

"Yes I am." He fiddled with his contraption.

"And me with the three days' worth of whiskers and the rat's nest of hair on my noggin."

"It's all part of the processing. Now look straight at me and don't move a muscle 'til I tell you."

I never did see the results, but they took that picture at the back end of things. They should have taken it when I entered the service and I was healthy and handsome.

From there I was led to the infirmary where I was measured and weighed. I'd shrunken down to five-feet eleven inches! When I enlisted, I was a strapping six-feet and three-quarters inch. The burden of sorrow has shortened me by nearly two inches. I weighed in at one-hundred-fifty pounds, down from the one-hundred-sixty-five last November.

Then the surgeon examined me from head to toe – peering into my peepers and my gullet, thumping my chest and belly, poking my ankles and feet, and inspecting my scars. Himself was an improvement over many an army surgeon I've encountered over the years, for there were no vapors of liquor coming off him and he had clear eyes, clean hands, and he spoke intelligibly. Finally, he held the wooden listening cup against my chest and instructed me to breathe as deeply as I was able. All I could muster was a painful wheeze before I was overcome by a lengthsome coughing fit which seemed to affirm his verdict.

Handing me a kerchief and furrowing his intelligent brow, he watched as I choked and gagged up the bloody catarrh then spit it into the cloth which I then swiped across my sullied lips. He reached for the soiled kerchief and tossed it into a bin of stained linens, then handed me three fresh ones.

"You will need to keep these always at hand. Once soiled, dispose of them in the canvas sack by the side of your bed for the orderly to gather. He will provide you with a fresh supply each day. I am sorry to say that your lungs are in rather poor shape."

"A holey mess is what they are," I gasped. "No need to mince your words, for I know I'm after drowning in my own blood and not long for this world."

His bright eyes turned soft. "Our goal is to make you as comfortable as possible. You will be dosed with opium twice daily to slacken the cough as well as the pain. I will instruct the orderly to provide you two extra pillows in order to raise your back and head while you rest. Be sure to use them at all times as this will keep pressure off of your lungs and aid in your breathing. With the deterioration of the lungs and the periods of fever, the appetite invariably suffers, but try at least to get the broth and eggs down as that will build up your blood and your strength."

I thanked him for his kindness, then an orderly shepherded me to a dormitory room with nine other fellas suffering differing levels of incapacitation. Though it smelled clean and the men lay on beds rather than cots, the room called to my mind the doleful wards at Cuyler and my heart took to galumphing in my breast. I felt the faintness coming on, but I girded myself to keep it at bay and followed the orderly thirty feet to my bed.

Relieved, I dropped down onto it as the orderly placed my satchel at my feet and left to fetch the extra pillows. Closing my eyes, I concentrated so deeply on the breathing and the gathering my wits about me that I barely noticed the orderly return and deposit the pillows at the head of my bed. Beyond startled I was when several minutes later a cheery voice intruded on my reverie.

"Welcome to Paradise."

I opened my eyes to the voice standing in front of me. It belonged to a big, one-armed, one-legged fella with a jolly red face. Demonstrating remarkable balance, he stood on the one leg with the aid of a crutch wedged 'neath his stub of an upper arm while extending the other hand to shake.

"Fred's my name, from the Nineteenth Wisconsin. I'm stationed in that bed beside you on the right."

"I'm Samuel from the Seventy-third Pennsylvania." I shook his hand and he proceeded to enlighten me on the particulars of the place.

"The victuals aren't bad. None of that damnable hardtack to crack your teeth on," he grinned as he patted his rotund belly. "Three meals a day and it's plenteous. We fellas all get along pretty good, mostly because aside from me, they don't talk much. Earl over there," he nodded across the way to a scrawny fella who appeared to be mesmerized by the ceiling, "he suffers awful from melancholia and fits, barely knows where he is. He's mostly quiet by day though he has spells of the judders, but he's a right loud screamer at night. If you're not too light a sleeper, you should get used to it in time."

The aforementioned Earl didn't seem to hear as he lay on his bed, gawping at the ceiling.

"Now Gus there on your other side, he's another one who never utters a word."

I turned and peered at the fella on my left. He looked to be fast asleep.

"Gus slumbers away most of the day and night, only wakes up to eat, piss, drop a shit, and when forced, to take the requisite weekly shower. Unless you see him walking to or from the dining hall or the latrine, you won't know he's around. Even whilst he's up he'll look neither left nor right so as to avoid any conversation. You'll find the rest of the fellas companionable enough, though we all have our oddities." He winked. "But you'll find that out for yourself in time. Now

I'd best let you settle in, but if there's anything you want to know about this place, I'm your man."

I thanked him. As he ambled away swinging his crutch with ease, I marveled at his cheerful state of mind what with his body so wrecked. As I pondered this, I proceeded to stow my few belongings into my footlocker. Then, since I had nothing better to do, I adjusted my pillows, sat on my bed and peered around.

Half of the beds were empty, their inhabitants presumably elsewhere. The remaining residents paid me little mind aside from the one or two who nodded in greeting.

I spied a dark-haired fella down the end of the dormitory with his snout deep inside a book. Driven mad with desire for the written word, I fairly scarpered down the room and approached him.

"I'm Samuel of the Seventy-third Pennsylvania," I extended my hand in greeting. "I've only just arrived here."

"Pete. Twenty-third Ohio," he mumbled without lifting his eyes from the page, continuing to read as if I didn't exist.

"Mighty sorry I am to bother you," I raised my voice as I dropped my hand, "but I was wondering if I could borrow that book when you've finished with it."

"No need," he murmured still absorbed in his reading. "You can get all the books you want from the libraries."

"*Libraries*? What are you on about, man?"

Pete deliberately lay his finger atop the page to mark his place and peered up at me, his eyes reflecting interest and dawning appreciation for a fellow booklover.

"Did no one tell you? We've two well-stocked libraries for our use. Putnam and Thomas Libraries are in the Headquarters Building, to either side on the second floor."

"Much obliged I am, Pete."

In a fit of ecstasy, off I hied to the main Headquarters Building as quickly as my holey lungs permitted me which seemed naught but snail-like to my book-frenzied brain. Once inside, I sat upon a bench, resting my lungs for several minutes before mounting the stairs to the second floor. As I peered up that staircase, I cursed the architects for their thoughtlessness toward all of us book-loving cripples!

When I had most of my wind back, I inched my way up those steps. 'Twas a laborious process which brought on the painful wheezing and the blackness of a faint. I fought the wooziness, clutching the banister as if 'twere a lifeline for that is what 'twas to me. When I finally reached the top, I waited for my head to clear.

What a celestial sight I beheld! To the east and west were portals to two libraries! I never thought to see such a sight outside of Philadelphia's grand library. I spent the rest of the day perusing the rows of books, all for the borrowing: Donne, Shakespeare and Milton, Dickens, Melville and Hawthorne, along with histories and nature studies. 'Twas then I knew I could find contentment here at The Soldiers' Home, and I thanked Attorney Poulson from the depths of my heart for arranging my stay.

And though the stairway to the second-floor libraries is a mountain to climb for my weary heart and lungs, 'tis always worth it. 'Tis with the rows of books I spend most of my days, away from the dormitory full of sorrowful broken men, away from my own melancholy misery.

Most days Pete accompanies me. We've become better acquainted and he's a fine fella. He's from stoical German farming stock and a bit stubborn, but loyal as the day is long. Once he's befriended you, he'll stick with you through thick and thin.

Pete suffers with the Irritable Heart too, as well as a crippled foot. 'Twas mangled by grapeshot at Antietam. He told me how he awoke on the field hospital table to see the surgeon grasping the saw just above his ankle. Pete cried out, "Put that saw down! You are not cutting me!" To which the surgeon responded that the foot was a sorry mess beyond repair, and he'd surely die of the gangrene if 'twasn't removed posthaste. But Pete would have none of it.

"I'd rather die all of a piece right now," he told that surgeon, "than spend my days bereft of my foot, unable to plow and tend my farm. Mend it as best you can, and I will take the consequences."

So 'tis half a foot Pete hobbles around on, but he says 'tis better than an entire wooden one. His farming days, alas, are over; he deeded his acreage over to his younger brother.

'Tis Fred who keeps the two of us from falling into our deepest melancholy. He senses when Pete or myself are heading into a bottomless brood. Despite half his limbs gone missing, Fred retains all his ebullient wits and sees it as his solemn duty to buoy our low spirits with his amusing anecdotes. He even makes light of his losing his limbs at Fair Oaks, saying whilst they're both gone on the one side and he may be unbalanced, if he stands side-wise with his good side facing you, you won't notice a thing. I suspect 'twas only due to his unfailing good humor that he survived such gruesome mangling and loss of blood.

'Tis fortunate indeed that we have Fred inhabiting our dormitory and lightening the mood with his antics. Gus is little more than a ghost in the bed beside mine, slumbering his days and nights away in silence. Poor Earl occupies his livelong days lying abed, silently weeping and gawping at the ceiling, whilst Pete and myself hobble down the libraries and find solace ensconced within the quietude and lovely aroma of paper, glue and leather binding.

Yet nighttime is unbearable for Pete and myself as well as poor Earl. We are fraught with the terrors and wake up screaming and sweating and trembling. Fred sleeps through it all like an innocent babe and wakes joyful to a new day.

William writes me regularly which is a comfort. And on the days when my lungs prevent me from traipsing to the libraries, Pete brings me the books. All in all, The Soldiers' Home is a haven where I can be unencumbered for a time from pain, from bother, from guilt, from an irksome wife. And though remembrances of my children distress me – their dear faces and fetching ways haunt me at odd times every day -- I suppress any blameworthiness, perpetually reminding myself they are far better off without me, who had become such an odious burden.

JULIA

'Tis a year now since himself run off like some lazy lump of a coward, waylaying his pension into the bargain. The state of him was so poorly, I can't help but think maybe he wandered into some alleyway and died like one of them drunken tramps. The coppers would've carted him off to a pauper's grave never to be found. God forgive me for being so cold-hearted but the truth of it is Samuel had no call to run off like that. I'd have seen to his care, bitter burden though he was.

Whatever has befallen Samuel was his fault entirely. Yet I must bear the shameful scandal. Tempted I am to call myself a widow, and who's to say I'd be wrong? Yet 'tis fear of damnation that keeps me from saying it aloud, for lawfully wed we was by a priest afore God.

My Sarah has me worried off my head. The poor thing has been pining so for her Pa all this past year with no abatement. The first couple of months whilst we was still living in Philadelphia, she'd sneak outside every chance she got and set on the bottom step in the freezing cold, keeping a lookout. 'Tis a miracle she never caught her death. Then all the while she was inside, she'd be heeding every creak and thump, running to check the stairway at every passing footstep.

In the Spring when I told her we was moving back here to Gloucester City, she nearly lost her wits.

"We can't leave here, Ma!" She fairly screeched. "Pa will never find us if we do!" She looked on me with that saucy reproving look I've become all too familiar with.

"He's left us no choice!" I bellowed back, tired of her making excuses for that rogue who threw us all to the wolves. "I can't be after paying the rent since he's took his pension money with him, since he gadded off without a care for any a one of us! And that includes youse little missy, so get that saucy look off your face and don't youse dare be after blaming me for that scoundrel's absconding! 'Twas only his own cowardly self he was after caring about."

My outburst undid her. She burst into tears, run out the door, down the stairs and out the yard. I let her go, hoping she'd see the awful truth in my harsh words and be shut of her worthless Pa. But 'twas all for naught.

She's still about the pining, which is doing her no good. Her wee face is always looking so mournful and she gets into broods like he did when she says nary a word, just keeps to herself. And there be times she gives me a sidewise black look for 'tis clear she still blames me for his leaving. When in truth 'twas him who come between me and my own child.

The others mention him but rarely. Jimmy and Mary seem right glad to be rid of him for they bear a grudge against him for his furious turning on me and his scaring of the wee ones. They're not his blood, so 'tis not surprising they show him no loyalty.

My poor lamb Kate is always away in foggy-dew land and notices nothing 'cepting what is right in front of her at the instant. She asked after him the day he left, and 'twas the end of it.

Eamon and Denny asked after him in the first few months, but I couldn't tell if 'twas on account of love or fear. Whatever the reason, they don't speak of him no more at all.

Maggie, barely three when he left, has forgotten him entirely.

SAMUEL

So feeble am I that I can barely hold a book, nor comprehend the words. 'Twas a sudden turning I took last week, no doubt due to the cold and damp of December. 'Tis hard to believe I've been here a scant four months, for I've settled in right grand with my comrades and my books.

'Tis been a month since I've been fit enough to hobble down the library. Pete's been bringing me the books, and grateful I am for his solicitude, but now 'tis hard work to read them for my mind strays. I find myself staring out the window at the gray clouds, the blowing bare trees and the falling snow, or I wake up of a sudden from slumber confused as to my surroundings.

Pete's taken to reading to me in the afternoons. He's a fine fella, a true friend. He's rarely left my side all week, but sits in the chair beside my bed, keeping me calm, seeing to my every need. I see the sadness and worry in his eyes, for we've become fast friends.

'Twill be hard on him when I go, especially since our cheery Fred up and died in his sleep of a sudden last week. Stone cold he was in his bed when morning came. His great heart just stopped beating whilst he slumbered. He deserved such a peaceful end, but we all fiercely miss him. Without him and his gladsome nattering, 'tis been like a morgue. 'Tis sorry I was not to be able to attend his burial, but I heard the mournful bugle announce it to all. When Pete came back, he gave me the particulars, and I pictured my own self's funeral which will be the next, no doubt.

'Tis grateful I am for the warmth of this place. I've been running the fevers and chills of late, so they moved me to a bed near the big-bellied stove which burns night and day. I'm down to one-hundred-forty pounds for I want nothing to do with food. They bring me broth and tea and with Pete's urging I struggle to get a bit of it down.

They've got me propped up with the pillows and are after giving me extra doses of opium to ease my breathing to no avail. My lungs can't hold the air since they're shredded and full of blood. I'm suffocating so I can barely cough, but when I do it's a rivulet of blood that flows up out my throat. On those frightful occasions when I'm flailing, Pete grabs hold around my back and heaves me forward to stop me drowning. He situates the pan 'neath my mouth to catch the flow, then rubs my back and says the soothing words 'til I've done with the dreadful spasms. Then he wipes the mess from my gob and tenderly resettles me upon my pile of pillows. I couldn't expect greater care from my own dear Mammy.

Doc Jewett comes to see me every morning, but he hasn't much to say. We look one another in the eye and 'tis clear we both know I'm knocking at death's very door. Though 'tis getting harder each day for me to speak, Doc Jewett is a patient man and listens attentively to my every utterance no matter the time it takes for me to do it.

This morning I fairly speared his eyes with mine, drew all my vigor into my enfeebled throat and said, "'Tis agony to be at this dying. Can you not leave me the full bottle of opium? 'Twould be a mercy."

He smiled sadly; my meaning was not lost on him.

"Though I sympathize wholeheartedly with you Samuel, and will do everything within my power to ease your suffering, I swore by my Hippocratic Oath to serve life not death."

"But 'tis not living I'm doing. 'Tis dying, and 'tis sorely frightening and painful."

"I'll order a stronger dose to relax your diaphragm muscles. That should ease you somewhat. It's all I can do."

I have to be content with what small mercies I am afforded.

JULIA

Poor Kate my innocent, my sweetest child, died two months past of the scarlet fever. 'Twas so quick, a matter of five days, from first flush of rash and fever to her passing. Thanks be to God the little dearie didn't suffer overmuch, just fell into a stupor and slipped away. Though I'll sorely miss her, 'tis better she's away safe in Heaven, for she was such a worry to me. What with her trusting, simple ways, she'd forever be the child in need of care.

Father Halloran, God bless him, saw to her burial. He supplied the pine coffin wherein my baby girl was laid after I bathed her for the last time and donned her in her beloved flowered frock. She looked the heavenly angel with her red-gold tresses curled about her pale freckly face. I'll keep that vision ever before me as a solace.

My others are after missing our Kate too, for she was ever merry. Without her to lift our spirits, there's a pall hanging about us, making us quiet and broody. Last month, my Sarah turned ten. She's after missing Kate something fierce, for them two, though opposite in outlook, had a special bond. Kate was the only one who could rouse Sarah from her worrying, melancholy broods.

And though 'tis been more than a year since her Pa left, Sarah's still beyond the beyond with the grief and cares naught but for her learning which takes her mind from her misery. She's no sooner in the door from a livelong day at school than she's got her nose in them books or she's writing the papers for to hand into the teacher next day. 'Tis a job I have of getting her to see to her chores which she does mighty poorly.

She cares not a whit about her appearance, barely drags a comb through her hair, but leaves it all in a tangle around her face, so's I have to pull it back and tie it with a ribbon to make her decent. Scolding her would just make things worse, so I try to turn a blind eye to her untidiness, but 'tis wearing on me for I'd die afore I'd let someone call me or mine Shanty Irish.

Meantime, my Mary and Jimmy are keeping the wolf from our door. I don't know what I'd do without them two angels of mine. I do worry after Jimmy's lungs, but 'tis naught I can do, for I need the both of their pays to keep us going. My Franky is married now with a baby on the way, so he can't be after giving us the odd bit of coin no more.

Though I'm taking in more laundering and sewing, it brings in but a pittance of what the seven of us needs, for the boyos is growing and are at the eating all the time. I'm forever running to the market for the eggs and the bacon and the wheat and the oats for to keep them filled up, for I'd not begrudge my children their food.

Fr. Halloran's cousin our landlord has been beyond generous in letting us the three large rooms for a price within our slim means. I suspect the good Father pays him a bit here and there to make it worth his while, which shames me something terrible. I never thought to be after accepting alms from the Church box.

SAMUEL

Father Werner arrived just minutes ago with the cold, gray dawn. He told me 'tis the twelfth of January. How he guessed I wanted to know I've no idea other than he's used to this death business, knows that a man needs to know his death date, his ending.

Amazed I am that I survived to see this new year of eighteen and seventy-nine. I'll not make forty-four years of age, but then I've known for a long time that I'd not make old bones.

I suffered a devil of a night, gasping and gagging and drowning. My man Pete sat beside my bed the livelong time, wiping my brow, sopping up the bloody flux each time it spewed up out my gob, rearranging my pillows to ease my struggle, tucking the covers about my shoulders. He sits here still, watching me like a devoted mammy with his swollen, exhausted eyes unabashedly seeping tears. Such a comfort he's been this last month, tending to my every need. I love him more than I can say.

Though utterly exhausted, I'm beyond restless and having a devil of a time trying to lie still so the good Father can finish his salvation business with the Extreme Unction. The poor fella is in all earnestness, clearly making a first-rate job of it to offset my lack of a worthy confession. Arrah, I came up with a few sins to please him, but then came the coughing and gasping, and then the great gushing of blood up out my raw, raggedy lungs, and I couldn't utter another solitary word.

Presently he's after signing the cross on my brow and hands with holy chrism. Like a second baptism 'tis. His voice is becoming a buzzing in my ear, hard to make out, but I think he's after saying he can't give me communion; the state I'm in I'd not get it down properly and might choke in the process. So he'll proceed with reciting the Apostle's Creed and the Our Father, and if I say them along with him in my heart, all my transgressions will be absolved.

According to my lights, I've transgressed far less than I've been transgressed upon. Besides, if there is a God -- and I like to think there is one who upon my arrival on the other side will enlighten me on why there is so much cruelty and sadness in this world -- He has more important duties than to tally up our failings. I am so very weary and so ready to go. I perceive with a serene certainty that I will be dead and buried before sunset this very day. I look forward to leaving all of my pain and sorrow behind.

The buzzing has stopped. I open my eyes to see Father Werner packing up his chrism, his candle, and his crucifix into his little black bag like as if he's a surgeon just finished up with his body mending. He smiles at me, pats my hand. I nod in thanks for his time.

As soon as Father Werner traipses off, I turn to Pete, my faithful friend. Feebly, I reach for his hand and he grabs ahold of mine and squeezes.

"Just close your eyes and be at peace, brother," he says through his tears. "I'll stay by your side 'til you go."

I nod my gratitude and close my eyes. I sink into the pillows and measure my breathing to the smallest possible inhalation. My lungs cease their struggling. My pain and restlessness recede. Soothing, warm darkness envelopes me.

A misty image appears. My children! Alive with their smiles, their lilting voices, the sweet smell coming off them. Lovely they are, and glad I am to have begotten them. I profess to them my everlasting love. They look on me with loving eyes as they fade away.

Back in the comforting, warm blackness, I float light as air. Then it's Mammy and Daddy to either side of me, clutching my hands, lifting me up and away into the light.

A MELANCHOLY UNION

PART THREE

AFTERMATH
1891

SARAH

Pa was gone ten years before we discovered his fate. And though a decade of daily struggle and grief is a long time, here I concern myself with only the crucial events that led to the unravelling of this mystery that hung over my family for so long. It was a strenuous time that is heartrending for me to recall. Yet I need to write it down in order to discern the truth, to clarify my mind, and to set my heart at ease before I can lay things to rest forever.

I cannot render this account in purely chronological order, for the memories return in random snippets which I must commit to paper as they come into my mind. I am determined to acknowledge all of my telling recollections, painful as they may be.

What haunts me most about Pa, the thing which soothes and saddens me equally, is his farewell. For I wonder sometimes was it just a dream? Yet it is crystal clear in my mind for I've gone over it thousands of times in the fourteen years since.

I awoke in the night to feel him gently stroking my cheek. The moon was brightly shining through the window, and I could see half of his face quite clearly. It was unbearably sorrowful yet abrim with love.

He whispered, "Please know that I love you, my wee *mavourneen*." And when I asked why he was up in the middle of the night in the cold and was he feeling sickly, he answered, "No *mavourneen*. I'm grand. I didn't mean to disrupt your sleep. Close your peepers and dream of lovely things."

Then he smiled most sorrowfully while his eyes welled with tears. He tenderly kissed my brow and tiptoed from the room. I recall that I felt a peculiar prickling at the back of my neck, a foreboding that he was bidding me farewell. He must have known I was listening to his every move, for I heard him settle back into his chair by the fire. Several minutes passed, and thinking that my foreboding was for naught, I resumed my slumber. Try as I might I cannot reconcile that final memory with what came afterwards.

When we awoke the next morning, Pa wasn't in his chair and Ma's face was a picture of worry. My neck prickled yet again as I inquired, "Where's Pa?"

"Down the jakes, most likely," she said not looking at me as she pulled the biscuits out of the oven. "Youse help the little ones with their breakfast now while I check on himself, see if he needs help with the stairs."

"I'll come with you, Ma," I told her as I followed her to the door.

"No, youse stay here and look after the little ones," she commanded as she hurried out the door, thwarting any argument by shutting it in my face.

I knew better than to follow her, but I opened the door and waited at the top of the landing while portentous fear gnawed at my insides like a ravenous rat. When Ma came back up the stairs alone, my dread turned to panic. I could see Ma's distress as she avoided my eyes and expounded some feeble excuse that maybe he'd simply gadded off down the tavern to fetch a newspaper.

But I knew better, knew beyond a doubt that he had absconded. I felt the truth of it way down in my bones. And I knew why. It was Ma's fault.

In my unbearable sorrow and perturbation, I accused her of driving him away due to her heartlessness in selling off his Daddy's books. She and I had further harsh words, and I defied her by running off to search for him. I couldn't stop myself, due to the agonizing state I was in.

I spent the livelong day frantically searching for him on all the surrounding streets and alleyways east to the river and then back west for a mile. All up and down Race, Front, Market, Chestnut, all the way south beyond Pine Street, and all the way up north to Callow Hill.

Although it was a dismally cold November day and I had rushed out without my coat, I barely felt the chill so intent was I on finding him. I would have continued through the night had my half-brother Jimmy not found me in the late afternoon and obliged me to come home with him, saying Ma was sick with worrying after me.

He'd brought a heavy woolen shawl which he wrapped about my head and shoulders and pulled me close to his side for warmth. But as we traipsed the long way back home, I began to shiver from the cold that had permeated to the very core of my bones. In my miserable state, I huddled against him and silently begged the Blessed Mother that upon our arrival home we'd find Pa sitting in his chair beside the fire, smiling in his sad way, telling me he was sorry for fretting me and setting his wee *mavourneen* off on a wild goose chase.

But it was not to be.

When Ma saw me, she threw her arms around me and nearly wept for joy. Then she sat me down, wrapped me up tightly in our best blanket and fed me hot soup and strong tea. Much to my amazement, in spite of my harsh words of parting from her that morning, she never scolded me for my rash tongue nor my disobedience. To the contrary, in the days to come she tenderly cared for me as she left me to my sorrowing. When I most needed it, she provided unstinting motherly devotion for which I will be forever grateful.

The first couple of years after Pa left were beyond painful for me. I never stopped hoping he'd come back to us, that he'd find us even after we'd moved back across the river to Gloucester City, for I'd left my heartfelt letter with our landlord who solemnly promised to deliver it to Pa should he return.

Every day I yearned to see Pa's tender, melancholy face and to hear his raspy voice, to feel his arm around my shoulders, his pat on my head. I even missed hearing his coughing, for it had been a constant in my life. The lack of it betokened the agonizing void.

I sharpened my ears and listened for every footfall outside our door. Every night I prayed to Our Blessed Mother to bring Pa safely home. I bargained with God, promising all sorts of things: that I'd never sass Ma nor pout; that I'd never lose patience with my little brothers and sister; that I'd be a bigger help to Ma with her chores. All for naught.

Eventually, I realized that Pa was gone for good. As a child of his heart, I could never accept that he had left us of his own choosing, for that would have meant that he hadn't loved me enough to stay. Consequently, I laid the blame at Ma's feet, that it was all on account of her betrayal of his trust.

After two years' time, I set aside my hope for a reunion. Pa's face slowly began to fade from my memory. I thought of him less and less until finally, a hardness set into my heart where the soft, hurt spot had been. I vowed to forget him if I could, like the rest of the family had done long before.

Almost as soon as he'd left, the others gave up on him with barely a qualm. Pa was a forbidden subject with Ma who only mentioned him when absolutely necessary and never with fondness. During the first few months after he disappeared, Eamon would occasionally ask me if I thought Pa would be coming back. I could see the hope in his eyes and I would hug him close and murmur lame assurances. But soon he was past caring. Meanwhile, little Denny all but closed his mind to Pa, and Maggie quickly forgot him altogether.

Two years after Pa disappeared, just after my eleventh birthday, Ma took me out of school so I could join Mary and Jimmy at the gingham mill. I was distressed to leave school for I loved learning, and the books were the only things that took my mind from my misery of losing Pa. Ma knew that, but she said she needed me to be earning money. She was always complaining about the lack, especially after Pa left, because we no longer got his "pittance of a pension" as she scathingly referred to it.

At the mill, I toiled as a spinner, standing all the livelong day at the spools, my feet and legs aching and my lungs smothering in the thick haze of lint. It was hard, dirty work, and it fouled my lungs so that I developed a perpetual cough. Dangerous too. I couldn't let my mind get to woolgathering for even a moment for those rapidly spinning spools were perilous to the fingers and would grasp and entangle anything hanging loosely about me such as a sleeve or more especially my long hair.

Every morning before we left home for the mill, Mary would meticulously pin up her own hair and then help me brush every single strand of my thick, heavy hair back from my face and pull it up on top of my head and pin it close 'til my scalp ached. Those were the mill's rules, for any loose strands of stray hair would surely find their way into the spools which spun so swiftly and forcefully, they could rip one's scalp clear off one's skull. Years before, Mary had been working right beside a girl who had failed to take the rules seriously and had let her hair come loose. She lost half of her scalp and nearly bled to death. I remember how Mary came home that evening, her tears streaming, her face haunted, her frock fouled and blood spattered.

Consequently, Ma took the extra precaution of wrapping each of our noggins tight with a kerchief. At first, I rued Ma's diligence for the spinning room was hot, especially in summer when my kerchief would become drenched in sweat. But then I saw for myself the horrendous consequences of not taking adequate precautions. One afternoon I heard a blood-curdling scream followed by the howling of a girl whom I could see was writhing on the floor, her head a gory mess. She bled so profusely that by the time they carried her out, the spinning room floor looked to be that of a slaughterhouse. That vision haunts me to this day.

Perhaps I should have resented Pa for leaving us without his pension support and forcing me to engage in such dangerous and dirty work at so tender an age, but it was Ma I felt bitter toward. I had always resisted casting blame on my beloved Pa, preferring to fault her for his leaving.

In truth, I had ample reason to do this. In addition to her betrayal of him, Ma was often cold and scathing toward him, accusing him of laziness and negligence when in fact he was seriously ailing. Refusing to accept the fact of Pa's mortal condition was a flaw in her character. And though she has always been a dutiful mother, she has a rigid coldness about her which I have always felt to be estranging. She could be particularly cold toward Pa who needed tender empathy.

Not that they never had any tender moments, for they did, especially when Pa was a-bed with the worst of the consumption. At those times, Ma went out of her way to bring him cups of strong tea with the extra milk she'd forego from her own cup, along with bowls of steaming broth, and a bit of scrambled egg with soda bread. She'd even help him with his spoon or fork when he was especially weak.

But most times she seemed indifferent toward Pa's suffering. When she sold his precious books, I think that exhibited a cold malice on Ma's part. Her deviousness shocked me, and it broke Pa who was already in bits beyond mending.

Hard as I try, it is impossible for me to be objective since I'm recalling this through my childhood perceptions, and I'd always been partial to Pa. We were close for we shared the same passionate temperament with our feelings roiling around just beneath our skins. He understood me while Ma never did. Pa was a melancholy man, in dire need of empathy. Affectionate, too. He was inclined to cuddle even when he was ailing, so throughout the day I'd embrace him tightly and tell him how I loved him more than anything in the world.

He'd hug me back and then give me his sad, crookedy smile, pat my cheek and tell me, "Ah Sarah, my wee *mavourneen*. What would I do without you who is always after bringing me the sunshine even on the most dismal of days?"

In contrast, Ma was standoffish, stern, and at all times completely practical. She had little time for cuddles or kisses for she was industrious to a fault and expected everyone else to be as busy as she who was always fretting about money and food and necessities.

I wish I had a picture of Pa, especially when he was hale and hearty. I only remember him as ailing and feeble, so to see him young and strong and donned in his sergeant uniform would be a blessing. I'm proud of his service for the Union Cause but angry that it cut his life short. Oftentimes I wonder how things would have been if he'd not been ailing. How different our family would have been if he'd been able to work steadily and survive to old age.

By the time I turned sixteen, I'd been working in the mill for five years. A year and a half prior, Mary had moved away from home to marry a fellow downstate in Salem. Then Jimmy got married and set up his own household which deprived us of his income. Consequently, my younger brother Eamon had to join me at the mill. The two of us were Ma's sole support, but Denny was twelve and would soon be joining us. I reckoned that as soon as he did, I would be able to leave the mill to follow my own plan.

I had been pondering my future for some time, and my prospects were limited. The customary inclination for women was to enter into marriage, but I didn't want any part of that. I'd seen what misery it brought: bickering and strife; insecurity and want; babies coming every other year wearing the body down; the ceaseless duty to them who needed to be fed and clothed. I'd seen the constant baby business not only with my own mother, but with the wives of my half-brothers Franky and Jimmy who were dropping babies nearly every year like cows.

More alarmingly, my half-sister Mary had nearly bled to death in the delivering of her first baby a mere ten months after her wedding. She remained pale and frail even six months on, and lived in constant fear of another pregnancy.

The other customary option for a young single woman was the going out to service as a domestic. However, those situations held risk and had to be scrutinized carefully. If you joined a reputable household, it was a golden opportunity to live in secure lodgings with plenteous food and a bit of money to call your own. Yet there were those unscrupulous folks who exploited their maids treating them as no better than slaves. I'd heard the priests' tales of girls being refused Sunday mornings leave to go to Mass and being cajoled to leave the Holy Faith and join the church of their Protestant employers. And of course, there was always the risk of being molested by the men of the house or beaten. Then where would one go?

There was, however, a third choice which I had been mulling over for some time. I had always esteemed the Dominican nuns who had taught me in school. I'd always admired their pursuit of learning and their sense of purpose. They didn't serve the whims of a husband or babies, but the precepts of God. I believed that following their life path would provide me intellectual and moral edification. It also seemed the surest path to Heaven.

I planned to go to the motherhouse of the Dominican Sisters of Hope to inquire about entering as soon as Denny took my place at the mill. In as much as Ma is such a devout Catholic, I thought she would be delighted with my decision, but when I told her, she was utterly dismayed.

"Youse will do no such thing! Them nuns are always after fasting from the the eggs and the milk! Why, they downright starve themselves!" she said. "And them convents are as damp and cold as the very grave for them nuns deprive themselves of firewood and coal so they're always suffering the chilblains, not to mention all sorts of lung ailments."

"My lungs would take it as a blessing to get away from the lint that's fouled them these last five years in that spinning room!" I retorted.

"I won't be listening to that lip of yours! Youse don't know what you're on about! Them sisters die young, for the starving and the cold brings on the consumption. God knows I am a true daughter of Holy Mother Church, but I am a mother to youse first and I'll not let youse enter a convent only to die there! Youse stay to home where you'll be sure of getting the egg every day."

Ma heartily believed that eggs warded off the consumption. No matter how dire our circumstances, we always had eggs because Ma, having made an agreement with our landlord to a share, kept half a dozen laying hens in a small coop in the yard.

Succumbing to her entreaties for the nonce, I remained toiling in the gingham mill. As time passed, however, my religious vocation waned and I stayed on at the mill for a further six years – all the while fouling my lungs with lint instead of Ma's dreaded convent consumption -- until this past November. That's when Ma was finally awarded her widow's pension with back pay. (The particulars leading up to this event will be revealed in due time.) Consequently, since Ma now received steady income, I gratefully quit the gingham mill. I went out to service with the Sanfords, a well-to-do family across the river in Philadelphia.

That was six months ago, and now in this year of our Lord eighteen-ninety-one, I am twenty-two years old and I have taken control of my destiny. As a live-in maid, I am at the beck and call of Mr. and Mrs. Sanford, yet I enjoy numerous benefits. I have my own private bedroom snug under the eaves of a grand house; I eat heartily of nutritious, fresh food; and I am able to save a bit of money into the bargain. I live in a teeming city full of interesting sights and people; I have Sundays off to do with as I please; and I am no longer under Ma's thumb. Peculiar as it may sound, as a domestic I enjoy a measure of personal freedom that ennobles and emboldens me.

In these past months since I've been away from home, I've been able to look back on our family's sorrowful history from a new vantage point of distance. Without Ma's persistent presence, I can ponder more clearly on all of those distressing years. Some things look different to me now.

I don't feel quite so harshly toward Ma. She has her foibles, but I realize she was always struggling to keep us all warm and fed. Considering her hardship as a girl back in Ireland enduring The Hunger, I can't fault her obsessive fear of deficient food and shelter for her children that renders her fanatical about money and security.

In retrospect, poor Pa seems all the more pitiful, so broken in body and spirit by that awful war. He was haunted night and day with nightmares of battles and dead comrades. His eyes revealed everything about what was going on in his body as well as his mind, for they were changeable depending on his physical and mental state. In his periods of relative wellness, they were a strikingly vivid blue. But as his periods of sickness came on, they dimmed to a lifeless gray. Yet, no matter the shade, they reflected eternal sorrow. He was deeply damaged, and for anyone, including Ma, to judge my Pa for any lack of ambition or manhood, to call him a malingerer, is to be in malicious error.

In spite of Pa's mournful feebleness, I remember some joyful moments we two enjoyed. As I mentioned, Pa was an affectionate man. He was also an avid reader who loved poetry, history, and natural science. Lacking access to books, in his perpetual curiosity he would read any newspaper or pamphlet that came to hand. What Ma called his "brooding" was often him engrossed in deep thinking about weighty matters she couldn't be bothered to ponder.

He loved his native land with a passion, and he would pull me up onto his knees and tell me tales of Ireland – happy stories and heroic fables – and he would engage his whole self in the telling. He'd make faces and change his voice, sing a little ditty. Of course, this was all before he became so intensely ill that final year or two before he disappeared.

While Ma taught me my Irish prayers *Se do bheatha a Mhuire, Ar nAthair,* and *An Gniomh Dolais*, Pa taught me the Irish songs *Sean O Duibhir a Ghleanna,* and *Fainne Geal an Lae.* His voice, when his lungs weren't troubling him too badly, was quite lovely, deeper than a tenor and sweetly sad. His singing was one of the things I missed most as his lungs deteriorated.

Whenever I am accosted by horrific memories of his lying a-bed and coughing up blood, I push them aside and call to mind his storytelling and his singing, for I think that was the true measure of my father.

Though a morally upstanding man, he wasn't religious. While Ma took us to Mass every Sunday, Holy Day, and First Friday, Pa only occasionally went. He blamed it on his poor health, but I think he wasn't always of the same mind as the Church. He seemed to distrust the priests and their teachings. I could read his doubts in his face which always gave away his feelings. This frightened me, because the nuns taught us that missing just one Sunday or Holy Day Mass would damn us to eternal hellfire. I worried so for Pa's sake that I asked him once about it.

"Ah my *mavourneen*, whilst your Mammy teaches you right by taking you to Sunday Mass, 'tis not my particular method for revering the Almighty. We have a different kind of affiliation, He and I. I close my eyes and then we two engage in the silent conversations. We understand one another just fine, so don't be after worrying about your Daddy's soul."

Although he seemed quite sure on this point it didn't soothe my worry, for the Catholic Church has strict rules which are not to be questioned nor bent for any reason. Consequently, every Sunday I spent the entire Mass praying for Pa's soul – which I continue to do to this very day because I hope that God in His mercy took into account Pa's terrible suffering and sent him to Purgatory for his missed Masses. There his soul will eventually be purified enough to ascend to Heaven.

So now I will explain how we found out about Pa's fate. After he had been gone nearly ten years, in the early summer of eighty-seven, my half-brother Jimmy decided to enquire into Pa's whereabouts on Ma's behalf. Jimmy hoped Ma was due benefits on Pa's military pension, especially if Pa had died which was entirely likely. Jimmy was twenty-four at this time, having worked his way up to being a clerk at the gingham mill where he tallied the accounts. It was a good job which paid fairly well, but by this time he had a wife and son to support and couldn't spare much to give Ma.

Jimmy is a clever man. Ma always said so, and it has always been obvious that he is her favorite child. While he is most like her in temperament, Ma's partiality is likely due to the fact that she holds an abiding fondness for Jimmy's long dead Pa, her first husband James Lyons. A fondness she never held toward my Pa, more's the pity.

Not surprisingly, Jimmy turned against my Pa after the alarming argument Pa and Ma had over her selling his Daddy's books. It was an awful scene to witness, far worse than any arguments they'd had before. I'd never seen Pa so riled and beside himself. He was so enraged that I feared he would strike Ma, and Jimmy clearly thought the same for he balled up his own fists and looked ready to accost Pa. It was only natural of course for a fourteen-year-old boy to defend his Ma. And though Pa never did become physically violent, the vile words he flung at Ma were enough for Jimmy to lose all respect for him. Jimmy didn't excuse Pa's righteous fury like I did. Ever afterwards Jimmy showed only cold eyes and silence toward Pa. When Pa left, Jimmy couldn't hide his relief.

I'm not sure how Jimmy went about enquiring into Pa's whereabouts, but sure enough on New Year's Eve of eighty-seven Ma received a letter from the government. Ma couldn't read nor write, so I always read what scant mail she received. I saw it was from the government and sensed it was the answer we were all awaiting. With trembling hands, I opened the letter and read it to Ma, my voice shaking the entire time.

It informed her that Pa had died on January twelfth, eighteen-seventy-nine. I had to stop reading for a moment to take this in. Pa had died a mere fourteen months after he'd left us. He'd been dead now for just shy of nine years! Though the affirmation of Pa's death saddened me, I wasn't surprised. What was surprising was what I read next. He had died and was buried clear out west in Dayton Ohio at a Soldiers' Home!

But my bafflement at his place of death was overshadowed by the terrible blow revealed at the end of the letter. When Pa had entered The Soldiers' Home, he had listed himself as *'Widower with no children'*, signifying his brother William as his closest relative. Consequently, though Ma claimed to be his widow, the records attested otherwise and she was not due any benefits.

Wounded to my very core, I tried to convince myself that there was some mistake, a mix up in identities, for Pa would never disown us. Besides, surely his brother William (of whom I had no recollection since we hadn't seen him since I was a wee babe) nevertheless would have informed Ma about Pa's death. But then, how could he have? He wouldn't have known where to contact us.

I asked Ma if she had any of Pa's military papers. She took a packet out of the bureau and sure enough, the service numbers matched. It was no mistake. Pa had not only abandoned us; he had disavowed us! This revelation broke my heart anew and kindled a heretofore unknown deep bitterness toward him.

While I was shattered, Ma was enraged. While I wept and struggled to come to grips with how Pa could betray his flesh and blood so heinously after having assured me of his love, Ma ranted and raved for days on end. I'd never seen her in such a lather. She even took to mumbling curses against Pa, which scandalized me no end.

Likewise, Jimmy was beyond infuriated at what he saw as Pa's perfidy. He immediately wrote to the rector of St. Mary's Church in Salem New Jersey, who responded with a certified statement that according to official church records, Samuel and Julia were married by the Reverend C. Cannon on March first, eighteen-sixty-eight in the presence of Michael Killian and Catherine O'Donnell.

Jimmy took this certification along with the government letter to Attorney Lockwood who filed Ma's claim for benefits on February second, eighteen-eighty-eight.

What followed was nearly three years of demeaning rigmarole. All sorts of past acquaintances had to be tracked down and affidavits had to be acquired from them attesting to the validity of my parents' marriage. They swore that there were no impediments; that Ma's previous marriage to Mr. Lyons had ended with his death in 1865; and that there were no subsequent marriages for either Ma or Pa. The baptismal records for all of us children also had to be acquired showing Ma and Pa as lawfully married.

More infuriating still, even though Pa had supplied all of the evidence regarding his war wounds and lung ailment that he had suffered during the war, this all had to be proved yet again via affidavits from army surgeons and fellow soldiers, all of whom had to be located twenty-five years after the events. Fortunately, enough of them were found still alive to make a case, but it was beyond clear that the government would make Ma fight for every penny she was due. If it hadn't been for Jimmy's tenacity and Attorney Lockwood's assistance, Ma would have been left completely wanting.

Throughout those three years of waiting, my bitterness toward Pa faded to sad disappointment. My love for Pa was too deep to allow me to deny my fondest memories. I would cherish those and push my resentment aside. The mystery of his disappearance was finally illuminated, so I could leave off brooding about him and focus on my future.

As I said earlier, I yearned to leave the mill behind me and to venture forth on my own.

Finally, a week before my twenty-second birthday, Ma received her letter informing her that her claim was approved. Two weeks later she received her back funds of $2,190 less $25 attorney's fees. In addition to that prodigious amount of money, she would receive a monthly pension of twelve dollars a month!

We were all elated. Upon receiving the funds, the first thing Ma did was thank Our Lord by purchasing two milk-glass vases for the high altar of our church -- St. Mary's in Gloucester City. It had just been rebuilt and dedicated the year before, and Ma was thrilled to donate something that would last. Every time we went to Mass thereafter, I could see her proud gaze settled on the vases.

Then with Jimmy's guidance, Ma bought her very own house farther down Cumberland Street, one block over from St. Mary's. It's a neat, narrow three-story where Ma and Maggie each have their own bedroom while my two brothers share the third one. Eamon is twenty and is a weaver at the mill while Denny, eighteen, is a spinner. As they moved down the street to the new house, I crossed the river to Philadelphia to take my position with the Sanford family.

Since Ma receives her regular pension now and money isn't tight, Maggie at sixteen can stay home. It's fortunate, since the poor thing has always been frail and excitable. She's as beautiful as a porcelain doll, but as fragile too, with her nervous headaches and stomach ailments, and abiding fears. It hasn't helped that we've all coddled her, but what else can you do for a loved one who is so vulnerable and delicate looking?

I'm working hard, grateful to Our Blessed Mother that she saw fit to guide me to a respectable position with a considerate family. I'm saving up my wages so I can take the train out to The Soldiers' Home in Dayton, a journey I must make in order to pay my respects to Pa and, hopefully, settle my remaining unease over his baffling conduct.

I need to see where Pa spent his last months, to visit his grave and be in proximity to his earthly remains. I know that aside from perhaps his brother William I will be his only kin to do him the honor, for the others have callously blotted him from their memories. Ma feels completely betrayed, and I can't say I blame her too much especially since she never understood Pa's true self.

And I can appreciate and sympathize with my younger siblings, since their recollections of Pa are vague due to them being so young when he absconded. Mostly, I think they are shielding their hearts from hurt, for God knows I have tried to do the same.

Yet even in my worst times, I never could shut my Pa out completely. Sweetly tender memories always leaked out from the depths of my heart and brimmed to the surface. He was an exceedingly sensitive, melancholy man, severely damaged in mind and body. Broken by circumstance, battle, and disease, he can't be judged by rigid standards.

I have been awash in conflicting emotions since my Pa left so many years ago. Yet I am hopeful that in Dayton in proximity with his spirit I will be illuminated as to his actions and state of mind so as to set my own mind at peace and mend my cleft heart.

I hope to lay aside my lingering anguish even as I lay a handful of daisies there at his headstone. Daisies were Pa's favorite flower.

A MELANCHOLY UNION

Glossary

acushla – pulse of my heart, darling

amadan – fool

An Gniomh Dolais – Act of Contrition

An Gorta Mor – The Great Hunger, the Irish potato famine of 1846-1852; also referred to as the Irish Holocaust in which one million died of disease and starvation.

aos si – faeries; malevolent spirits who live in mounds or trees, who must be avoided and appeased to prevent them from stealing pretty babies and replacing them with peculiar changelings

Ar nAthair – Our Father

banshee – mythological female spirit who foretells death by a loud, eerie keening or shrieking

blaggard – blackguard, scoundrel, villain

bodhran – round, hand-held drum, thumped by hand or with a bone tipper

boxty -- potato pancake

cess – a tax or military assessment

ciotog – left-handed person

colcannon – a mixture of mashed potatoes, cabbage, milk, butter, and onion

eejit -- idiot

gob – mouth

gone in his cups - drunk

long in the tooth -- old

louser – mean, nasty, disreputable man

mavourneen – my darling, my sweetheart

oxter -- armpit

pratie – potato

Sasanaigh – Saxons, English intruders, overlords

seanchaidhe – traditional storyteller of familial lore

secesh – secessionists, rebels

Se do bheatha a Mhuire – Hail Mary

scalp – a hole dug in the ground, covered by straw or sod

spalpeen – impish boy, rascal, scamp

three sheets to the wind - drunk